Bass Instinct

Bass Instinct

A Novel

Two Fingas

Published by Repeater Books

An imprint of Watkins Media Ltd

Unit 11 Shepperton House

89-93 Shepperton Road

London

N1 3DF

United Kingdom

www.repeaterbooks.com

A Repeater Books paperback original 2025

1

Distributed in the United States by Random House, Inc., New York.

ISBN: 9781915672964

Ebook ISBN: 9781915672971

The manufacturer's authorised representative in the EU for product safety is: eucomply OÜ - Pärnu mnt 139b-14, 11317 Tallinn, Estonia, hello@eucompliancepartner.com, www.eucompliancepartner.com

Printed and bound by CPI Group (UK) Ltd, Croydon, CR0 4YY

Contents

Prologue

I was born in St Thomas' Hospital, South London, of a Jamaican father and a bi-racial mother. My mother was born of a Scottish mother and a Bajan father. My sister Juliette's father was white, an engineer. She's four years older than me, she's just finished her degree. I grew up in South London, moving between Vauxhall, Clapham and Brixton.

1982 was a watershed of a year for me, it was when I saw my first world cup. When I changed the name that I had been given at birth to one that I would use for the rest of my life. But more than that, 1982 was when I fell in love with music, when I knew without any shadow of a doubt what I wanted to do with the rest of my life.

I wanted to be a DJ.

I wanted to own a record collection so large and diverse that it would put a museum to shame. I knew that that was what I wanted to do as soon as I heard the TUNE. I wanted to play songs like that, to make songs like that. I wanted to leave a mark on the world through the music that I played.

I didn't know what DJing involved, but I knew I wanted to do it. To affect others as I had been affected.

Back in the dark days before science demystified everything, people believed that the sun and the other planets revolved around the earth and that when they were synchronised they created a heavenly music. The music of the spheres. A melody so beguiling that humans would do anything to listen to it again.

When I was eleven, I heard it, and ever since I've been searching for it.

Side One

July

Summer Breeze

The sun slides slowly over the horizon, smooth and golden. As its rays brush past the feeble defences of the night. Stretching forth gloriously unruffled and honey slow. No need to rush. No need to worry. Sol around which everything else revolves. Rising high in the Clapham sky. Gleaming spires radiating light, morse-code beacons. As the sun reflects and refracts. Diamond sparklets as the rays roll inexorably on.

The rays cut through my half-closed curtains, long beams of light, solid in the early morning gloom. Solid and tangible. Able to bar your path, stop forward motion. Small particles of dust caught within them, as if flies in amber. Transfixed for the longest time. Held in stasis until the sun lowers itself back under the horizon. Then they become free to float again, drifting aimlessly through the moonbeams and the flickering sodium glare of the streetlights.

She moves softly against me and nuzzles closer, seeking warmth or comfort. This day will be hotter than yesterday, and the day before that, and the day before that. The thin cotton sheet pulled up tight beneath her. The long folds of the fabric stretching away, creating a microcosm of peaks and valleys. A strange cross-section cut out of the ocean floor, of planes and levels of definition. As the shadows cast across her slowly change as the sun moves higher into the sky. Affected not only by that movement but also the movement of her body beneath it. The fluidity of the fabric as it smoothes her motions into a dance of zero-gravity gentleness. Flowing around her, beneath her, over her. The repetition of the words only solidifying the essence of her movement.

I look at her face, calm in repose, so unlike the intensity of facial expression that danced across it before. Now she is childlike and I feel the urge to protect her, to keep her safe from the harm that waits outside the window. Along with the hard intensity of the sun's gaze.

She rolls, her arm moving swiftly as she flips the sheet off her, exposing herself. The innocence and the unconsciousness of it make me grow hard in an instant. Stiff and uncomfortable as I watch the light turn her into a golden statue. The hair that covers her face concealing her eyes, whilst that softer, gentler hair, cut into a sharp V, is revealed as she lays on her side. I haven't known her long enough to be comfortable with her lying on my bed. Actually, I've only known her a couple of weeks. This is the first time that we've fucked. Banged, boned, popped it, dug it. I don't call it making love anymore. That's too wrapped up in conventional society's hang-ups and my own personal misgivings for the physicality of the act that we shared. I prefer fucking now. Fucking is what I do now. Making love no matter how tempting or beguiling holds too many dangers. I may risk my life in many ways, but I won't risk my sanity. The emotional ties that swim up out of the ether and surround you before you have time to react hold no attraction for me.

I slip out of bed and scratch my bollocks, a morning ritual I've never been able to shake myself out of, and survey my room. In the estate-agent blurb it said it was twenty by twenty-four feet, but I've measured it, and even though the numbers were the same, it still feels small. Maybe it's just the amount of stuff I've got crammed into it. I'm always surprised by the amount of stuff and junk I've accumulated in my twenty-two short sentient years.

The floor's covered with my clothes and socks, both half worn, as in once or twice. Once they're worn three times, they're dirty and head for the laundry basket behind the door so they can be washed. Various boots and trainers lie like mines planted just underneath the surface waiting to trip you up and explode that cultivated air of cool. Sending you hurtling back to childhood inadequacies, when you couldn't make your limbs do what you wanted them to.

The best thing about my room, apart from it being mine and having my set in it, is the huge south-facing window which catches all of the day's rays. A huge one-piece pane which tilts to open.

Flop down onto one of the three director's chairs strategically placed for visitors and pull the skins and grass which lie on a flat piece of marble which a friend gave me. It's about eighteen inches square and you're supposed to put your deck on it to eliminate any vibrations from reaching it so you get a purer cleaner sound. A load of fucking knob, but audiophiles will go to any lengths to get better sound. Me I just use it to skin-up on. Usually I have a few spliffs pre-rolled so I don't have the hassle of skinning-up every time I want to burn. I carry them round in an old silver cigarette holder that I brought for a tenner off this woman on a stall in Camden, just over the lock. It's got an elaborate coat of arms engraved on the front. Two unicorns rearing up over a shield with some Latin underneath which she told me translated to "At the eye of the storm". When you flip it open you see an inscription which reads, "No man knows the mysteries of the human heart as well as a woman. To my darling Georgina."

She was a frail old woman, with eyes that were sharp blue.

Birdlike in that they stared intently at you and didn't waver or blink. The skin across her hands was translucent and you could see the veins beneath working like nutters. But she gripped my wrist so tight that memories of Chinese burns came rushing back. She wouldn't let go until I brought it. She had a way of speaking, clipping words and shortening them as if she didn't have enough time, as if everything must be done quickly. The intensity of her fascinated me. So much power contained within such a small, fragile vessel. Even after I bought it, I'd come back every few weeks just to sit and watch her selling her old silver trinkets. Knick-knacks, all of them. Whether they were personal or not I don't know. But she would grab others with the same intensity with which she grabbed me. I could see the way people would be drawn to her, by that odd diction that carried over the noise of the market.

The merging of sounds, of tapes being played by vendors, the clashing of voices, accents from around London and then the spitting cadence of the Spanish or the Arabic and then the soft rolling vowels of the Irish or the Scottish. The hard beat of Belgian house rolling over you as a BMW weighted down with speakers designed for home use wedged into the back passed you by. Stall holders haggling with customers some refusing to budge, others more compliant, more willing to enter into negotiations. But through it all, that voice. Not loud, just there, cutting through it all. Calling people to buy her wares.

I take out a few skins and quickly roll up. My fingers dry and white, reminding me that I have to buy some more cream. My nails are long and should be clipped, but it just makes it so much easier to roll if my nails are longer than I would like. Pull out my trusted old clipper and take out the flint stick. Well that's what Jade calls it. Tap down the tobacco until it's flat and level, and twist, letting the grooves take hold of the paper, and wind it round it. Making it nice and neat. Pop it back in and flick the wheel. I let the flame gently lick across the paper around the pointed end until it falls off into the small ashtray by my feet and the end glows red. Sit back and drag on it. Holding the smoke deep in my chest before trying unsuccessfully to blow smoke rings through the shafts of sunlight that slant across my room. Adjust my position in the chair and relax.

Feel the smoke linger in my lungs as I draw again. Imagining the THC filtering through my system. Feel my body go cold as the weed runs through me. My bare skin feeling every waft and draft of air. Pull on it again and tap ash off gently into the ashtray. Tap tap, either flick it with your thumb or knock it with your forefinger. Hold the spliff away from my face as I rest my head on my hand and watch the smoke drifting into the air. Cool grey vapour.

I watch her and try to figure out why her being here makes me uncomfortable. Why the fact that she lies in my bed makes me squirm as if my mum's interrogating me about the stack of porno mags under my bed. I gaze at her and wonder, why me? What attracted her to me and not to anyone else.

I gaze at her and I wonder. Her breathing deep and sure, breasts rising and falling. Her rib cage visible. Flesh stretched taut over bone. So fragile. Take another deep drag and blow smoke back into the atmosphere. My body already relaxing as I sink ever deeper into this haze. This shimmering, shifting feeling as the smoke slides through me. Take another quick drag, feeling the heat of the tip as I pull on the roach. Close my eyes to avoid the smoke and breathe it back out. Drop the roach into the ashtray and step back towards the bed with that intense concentration known only to drunks, babies and people that get stoned. When walking towards your bed from the other side of the room becomes an act of the utmost importance and solemnity. When total and utter concentration is required to sustain mobility and forward motion. My limbs feel disconnected from me, my brain signals taking a split second longer to be processed and carried out. Making movement exaggerated and jerky.

Moving forwards in this *Thunderbird* parody I feel a dry, tacky connection between my foot and the stripped wood floor, varnished to a gleaming sheen where it isn't covered by clothes. Steady myself as I contort my body to see what it is and take it off.

Used condom, now a pale blue. Five ridges along its length. Arouser for her pleasure. Dried semen, vaginal juice and spermicide coat its length. Pull it off my foot and sling it towards the bin. Whether it goes in or not I don't know, I'm already angling for the bed. Crawling over it gently so as not to wake her. Bend my face over her as I watch the soft hairs lying along her cheek moving gently. Blow softly across them, watching them shift and sway. Lie down, slipping under the sheet and adjust my position to her. My groin against her butt, my arm across her breasts. Tug her nipple delicately with my fingers, roll it clockwise then anti-clockwise. Feel it harden and stiffen. God, I love breasts. Kiss her neck, snuggle close and lower my lids. Run my hand down across her stomach and let my finger nestle in her belly button.

Fantasy

"You know what I love?"

"What?"

"I love it when you see your cum rolling down a girl's inner thigh and her pussy glistens from both of your juices combined."

"I'm too nice for that sort of thing."

"You still wearing rubber johnny?"

"Damn skippy. I ain't down to be catching nothing. I ain't visiting the clinic again."

"Listen, I ain't going back there, but nothing can beat the feeling of it going in bare. So much sensation. Feels as if you're going to cum right there and then. But you hold it."

"Okay!"

"Not just okay, better than okay, fucking okay would be a better way to describe it."

I hand Iago the spliff and feel myself drifting away.

"What's the best sex that you've ever had?"

"The sex that I ain't had yet."

"No, seriously."

"Well…"

Iago starts to lean back and rock, going into his old-man-of-the-sea routine. Talking as if he's lived a lifetime already.

"Best sex, it's difficult, there's been so many."

"Yeah, sooooo many!"

"Well there was Julia. We had sex standing up in the back of a club. She was four inches shorter than I was. Damn was that difficult. We had to stop every time someone came past.

Just the illicitness of it was enough. My legs were trembling, I couldn't breathe properly, we were making so much noise I was certain someone was bound to hear us. But that was the beauty of it, that fear of discovery made it all the more exciting. Makes me horny just thinking about it."

"Ever done it again?"

"Nah, it was one of those spontaneous things that just took off. Right girl, right time and all that. Most girls are pretty prudish and unless it's in a bed or somewhere where they feel comfortable, they ain't going for it. So you can rule out toilets, buses, trains, the back seat of your car and anywhere outdoors."

Iago takes another deep puff and hands the spliff back to me. The small room in which we're sitting quickly filling up with smoke.

"But then again there's also the time Angela sucked me off. Now that was gorgeous. I mean totally inspirational. You know, she just got on her knees, as if she was going to pray. Took my dick out and started to blow me. I thought I was going to die or something, because it was pitch black and I could only feel her tongue. I just made gibbering sounds and clutched at her hair."

"Did she swallow?"

"Yep. Took it all, and at the end all I felt was a continuous shiver along my spine, just running down towards my butt."

We sit in silence as I watch Iago roll another spliff and try to ease the stiffness in his pants from remembering the experience. While I finish off the one in my hand. Pull on it hard and then grind it out in the ashtray whilst blowing smoke into the rafters.

"Best sex I ever had is a tie between the first time with Emma and this one time with Eve."

I smile at the memory of them.

"It was our first time, both virgins, and it was so… you know… awkward and hasty, and over too soon. But it was like, like… It was like a revelation. This is what it's like. Finally I know what sex is about. It was so weird you know just where I had to slip it in, not wanting to hurt, not knowing what I was doing. She was scared, I was scared. She was crying all the way through. Fuckin' scared me. Thought I was killing her or really hurting her. The amount of times I stopped and asked her what was wrong and she didn't answer, just pulled me back inside her. I come, don't know how the fuck she's feeling. Then she reaches up and whispers in my ear that it was wonderful, beautiful. And I feel as if I'm ten feet tall. Like nothing on earth can touch me."

Reach down and take a quick swig from the bottle of K on the floor beside me as I lie on the rapidly settling bean bag, and Iago rocks on the rocking chair across the way.

"Then there was Eve."

My voice breaks a bit when I think of Eve. She's gone now, gone. But I still think of her, that warm body beside mine, the way that she would play with my hair, run her fingers through it. My stomach still churns away when I think of her, the way it would do whenever I saw her. She always took my breath away. I was always wondering how such a gorgeous creature was going out with me. Was she stupid or something. Blind. Maybe she was just taking pity on me. I don't know. But I loved her, I still do. I still have every letter she wrote me, but I know if I bring them out and read them I'll break wide open and the pain will never go away. Right now I can carry on with my life if I just don't think about her, but she's always there at the back of my mind.

"Eve! We were at her friends, Irene's, she was staying there while she found a new place. Irene's sister Josephine had brought some cheesecake knowing that Eve loved it and was cutting it in the front room. We were going out straight after and Eve wanted to change and we fucked right there on the bed. Half dressed, her pants down by her ankles, my pants by my ankles. Both laughing our heads off. Halfway through I had to step inside her trousers so that she could bring her knees up. It was so intense. Just so intense. We could have sworn they must have been able to hear us, because we got some weird looks when we came out. But the thing was it couldn't have lasted more than five, maybe ten minutes, but they were so intense it was like my skull was exploding when I came."

Iago passes across the spliff and now it's my turn to shift, while my erection subsides and becomes less painful and awkward.

"You know what I love?"

"What?"

"I love a woman who's not self-conscious about her body or her sexuality."

"Few and far between."

"I know, but there's something about a woman who's got the confidence to be comfortable with you looking at her naked. You know, not be worried about her appearance.

"You mean when she gets out of bed after you've just been boning, totally bare-ass naked and she don't care that you're staring at her butt or her breasts or her stomach."

"Exactly. She's not worried about being too fat or too thin, or that she's got a slight pot belly, or that her butt's not as firm as it might be."

"You know what's even better, when a woman desires you and makes no bones about it. Doesn't try and hide, but just let's it be known that she wants you in the worst possible way, now that is exciting, and such a boost to the ego. None of that playing behind 'I'm a girl, come and get me.'"

"You know what I love about summer?"

"Hot pants, tight T-shirts, non-bra-wearing women, Lycra, short skirts. What?"

"All of those, but I love lying naked after sex and not having to pull the covers over you because it's summer and it's hot all the time. That's what I love."

"I'd like to fuck Lisa I'anson."

"Halle Berry."

"Tyra Banks."

"Jada Pinkett."

"Naomi Campbell."

Screw up my face, twist up my lip.

"Maybe."

Iago starts to sing, low and deep, doing the rolling background sound as well.

"Dreams of fucking an R'n'B bitch."

"You got that?"

"Damn fucking skippy. Had-to-have, must-buy-at-all-costs tune."

There's a creaking and light streaks up into the dimly lit attic room.

"Hope you didn't miss me."

Khadija runs quickly up the ladder and closes the door behind her to keep as much of the smoke as possible in the room and not let it filter down to her parents beneath. She takes her seat beside us and Iago hands over the spliff. Khadija's the bong queen of the universe. When I first met her she wouldn't smoke unless she was using a bong. Because none of us had any bongs, she would go around making bongs out of plastic bottles, traffic cones, any and everything.

"So what were you talking about while I was gone?"

"Girls."

"Fucking."

"Best sex."

"You know, man talk."

"Yeah, I know."

"Hey, you wanted to know."

"But it's like if you're not talking about sex or women, you're talking about records and hi-fi or you're talking about bikes or playing out."

"I don't talk about bikes."

"Okay, cars then."

"Thank you."

"Don't you ever talk about anything else?"

We look at each other, then turn back to Khadija.

"No."

"I didn't think so."

"Where's your sister?"

"Out with her friends, if you can call them that."

"I had visions of her being here smoking with us."

"Like fuck."

"I take it you and your sister don't get along?"

"We get along fine just as long as we're not in the same room for too long."

"So, Khadija, what was the best sex you ever had?"

She takes a quick puff on the spliff, taking a lot in, then holding before blowing it out.

"Best sex, hmmm, let me see."

"We don't have all night."

"Yes, you do."

"Okay, so we do, just a figure of speech."

"I can't say. All of it was good."

"Don't come with that, best sex ever."

"It's different for women. Some sex is purely physical. I want to fuck and that's it. But then there's sex where you're emotionally tied into them and it just feels as if you want to rip open your chest and swallow that person lying on top of you up. That even though you're as close as two people can be during sex, you still want to be closer. That no matter how deep he goes inside you, you want him to go deeper and deeper."

"Shit!"

"Now if we're talking positions. I like to be on top, sitting on his lap. You just have more control over how fast and how deep."

"Pass that spliff over, you been hogging it all night long."

"Oh, sorry."

Khadija hands it over and it's getting pretty close to the roach, so I gesture for her to make another one. Despite her proficiency with making everyday household objects into bongs, Khadija has little skill in the art of skinning-up. Sometimes I wonder why I even ask her to try. But if that horse kicks you off, you gotta dust yourself down and get back in the saddle. So I keep forcing her to try and try again, no matter how horrific the final product. Which inevitably I have to repair. I stub out the roach.

"Give it here."

My fingers flying as I skin-up very quickly. Just to really make her feel inadequate.

"What's it like giving a blow job?"

"Why'd you want to know?"

"It's one of those taboo questions that men aren't supposed to ask. You know, if you want to know the answer, you're harbouring ideas about doing it. Therefore you are homosexual. So what's it like?"

"It's like eating an ice cream without biting huge chunks out of it. I get a thrill out of it. When whoever he is is shuddering and moaning. I don't know, you can't really explain it. Some girls like to, others don't. I think a lot of girls don't like to be forced into it. Guys just shove their heads down there and say suck, when it ain't like that. You have to be more considerate than that. I see sex as a partnership. Pleasure is as much about giving as receiving."

I light my spliff and puff deep on it, quickly slipping back into my drug-induced haze.

"What do you fantasise about?"

"Er! Give me a minute to think about it. Tell me yours while I'm thinking."

"I fantasise about twins, and breasts. Suffocating in a sea of breasts. All of them just surrounding me. Breasts all around. Swimming through them and sucking on them, feeling them harden in my mouth. Just grow stiff, when I lick them."

I demonstrate with my tongue, rolling it in the smoke-filled air, tasting the weed on it.

"Breasts and twins, that's what I fantasise about."

Summer Madness

I sit naked on my bed and listen to the soft scratch of the wind as it slides against my net curtain. The net rustling and moving as the breeze slants gently against it. It's still hot like a motherfucker. Scorching, blazing heat that drives out all sense of reality, of propriety. How many other times would I sit naked and alone in my room, wondering whether I should try and grab some time standing in front of the open doors of my fridge. Instead I grab an ice cube from the rapidly melting pile by my thigh and slowly roll it across my chest. Sharp intake of breath as my skin, which feels as if it's on fire, is quickly cooled. For a few seconds while I rub the ice cube along my flesh, I feel relatively stable and normal. But not for long, as the heat of this month overpowers it and leaves me once more feeling hot and oppressed, with nothing I can do about it.

My eyes are slits, my breath is shallow. I drop the cube back into the bowl, what's left of it anyway. Smearing the remaining liquid on my fingers across my face. Shift my butt on the towel spread there. It's early evening, just gone half six and I'm wondering why it isn't getting any cooler. The sun's sliding down over the horizon and my window's as open as it can be. But I still can't find any wind. The Isley Brothers were chatting shit about summer breeze. Fuckers sure didn't live in London.

I get tired of sitting on my arse, so I stand and stretch until my spine creaks and pops and my chest makes an almighty cracking sound. I haven't done shit all day. Working a three-day week gives you a different outlook on things. Lean against the open window and look down out onto the grass beneath. It's too small to be a common and not big enough to be a park. I remember cutting across there with the other kids, still in school. So much energy, stripping off our shirts and screaming like madmen. Voices raised so everyone could hear. That warbling rising wail that we produced as we ran passed down from generation to generation, so now kids who I don't know do it. It was a badge of identity, a way of belonging. So we'd play football into the night, the sun slipping away, the light fading. Mothers leaning out on balconies yelling for their offspring to come home. I was one of the few, the brave, the few whose mother wouldn't call for me. We knew that we were in deep shit. So we'd stay out as long as possible, delaying the inevitable. Those kids whose mums would call, their voices becoming more and more frantic as the night wore on, knew they were safe. They could tell just how long to stretch it, until just when she was about to come down and look for them, they would appear out of the dark. Teeth grinning and duck out, heading home. But us whose mothers didn't call, we never knew whether our mums would let us slide or make us pay for keeping them in suspense and staying out so late when we knew what time we were supposed to come in.

My mother wasn't one to beat me often, but when she did, I remembered it. Her accent would thicken, become more pronounced, that Scottish brogue stepping forth. It would become just like Granny's as her hand flashed down upon me. She'd never come at me direct, always obtusely, laterally. There'd be no shouting in our house when I was getting beat down, just me crying long and hard. My cries of anguish turning into whimpering pleas for mercy. She'd beat me fierce. The hand falling forever. Time would stop when Mum beat me. There would just be the pain across my thighs, spreading outward as my skin reddened. After the first few blows I'd stop twisting in her grasp and just stand there, trying to go beyond the pain, but unable to. And Mum, grim as death, standing there over me. She never trotted out any of the cliches that my friends would recite at school. Another black experience that white people would just never understand. They would laugh and joke, voices raised high as the tube rocked through the blackness. The bulbs above us occasionally flickering to remind us that we were in a tunnel miles beneath the earth. That this wasn't sunlight above us, but hard, harsh, artificial lighting that could be switched off at any time, plunging us into unremitting darkness. They would laugh and the accents would come out, thick Jamaican accents, rolling forth over the roughness of our London twang.

"If you can't hear, you shall feel."

"What you crying for. I'll give you something to cry for."

Bursting into laughter at each example, a chorus of voices expanding through the carriage. Each with a new angle, a new variation on the getting-beat-by-Mum theme. I'd listen and I'd laugh but I would never add my story. Because Mum wasn't like that. She'd just hit me cold and remorseless. No sound coming from her except just before the first blow would fall, when she'd tell me why I was getting beat. With her accent growing stronger by the second.

After the beating she would send me to my room and I'd dive onto my bed and cry into my pillow, and sometimes I could hear her crying out in the hall. Her sobs muffled because she had her face in her hands, and I'd wonder what's she crying for, I'm the one who just got beat. My heart would harden and I'd pray that I was adopted and that soon my real parents would descend like angels to take me away from this living hell.

But shit like that don't happen, so I'd go to sleep and wake up in the morning and everything would be like it never happened. Life just rolled on. Summer. Winter. School. Mum would make breakfast and then duck out to work, and I'd sit in front of the TV for a while watching *Why Don't You?* before ducking out for another day running through the long grass. Playing British bulldog, screaming, yelling, sweating. Knees scraped, my trainers talking to me. Scarred, bruised and tired, but triumphant. I would return aware that I had to be on time this time. Slip in just before my curfew and watch while Mum pulled my food out of the oven.

I watch the shadows lengthen, the softness that has enveloped my part of town. The light being cast no longer defining, forcing things apart, but now blurring the edges, making forms and shapes melt together, soft like Haagen-Dazs that's been left out overnight. The sky now a gentle pink, the cutting blue that it is during the day spooling into the pink all around.

I stand by the window for a long time and just stare, my eyes becoming unfocused, seeing but not seeing at the same time. Two states of being combined at the same time. Time passes slowly, how much I'm not sure. A minute, fifteen maybe. I can't tell by the sky or the amount of light that passes by my eye.

Lean out of the window and stare at the brown grass beneath, feel it flex and bulge as if the floor is aware of my looking at it and is changing its perception of itself. Imagine myself falling towards it, falling, falling. Aware and awake of every second of my flight. My velocity increasing, pushing me into an inevitable collision.

I'm snapped out of my staring game with the earth by the coarse sound of the phone ringing. It coughs loudly into the silence, unwilling to be unnoticed, forcing me to pay attention to it.

"Hello…"

"You ready?"

"Once I put on some clothes."

"Hurry up, I'll be there in fifteen minutes."

"No, you won't."

"Time me. Later."

"Later."

I hold the phone for a few seconds after Iago's put his end down. Hearing the dead tone, the dead air between us. Phones are so impersonal, detached. You have no idea what's going on inside the other person's head. What emotions they're feeling. Whether they're happy or sad, or what. You've just got to go on the sound of their voice. No eye contact, no facial expression, just on the words that they say to you and the tone that they say those words in. So much is open to misinterpretation, misunderstanding.

I put the phone down and ponder on what I should wear tonight. I know what I'm going to play; all of my records are stacked and boxed in their flight cases, all ready to go. Just waiting for me to pick them up and shove 'em into the back seat of Iago's Mini. Look over to my clothes rail standing up against the wall. Stuffed full of shirts and tops, jeans and jackets. To brief or not to brief that is the question. Pull out some boxers and drag them on. Pull on my Jean shorts and then look to my wall, where they hang. The special wooden pegs varnished and gleaming on the bare white wall. Their backs to me, the numbers the same even though the colours are different. When I put them on, I know what I was put on this earth to do. I know who I am and why I am. No doubts enter my mind. I slide my hand over the fabric, lifting it to my face and inhaling of the fragrance. The fabric's starting to fade, but still, to me, it has a lustre all of its own. Brazilian shirts have a magic that no one can deny. I pull it on and feel reborn, the yellow fabric taking on a luminescent glow, everything spins into slow motion, *Raging Bull* black and white, except for the glowing Brazilian shirt. Slip my arms through the sleeves, the fabric rubbing over my bare nipples. Pull my head through and roll it down across my stomach, knowing that I am Eder, the boy from Brazil.

Push my hands into the deep pockets of my shorts and play with my bollocks, then pull them out as I sit to pull on my Air Max. The wooden frame of the bed comes courtesy of Granny. I broke the old one jumping on it, pretending to be spiderman or something, had to sleep on a mattress on the floor for ages until Granny came down for a visit, bringing with her some geezer from the old country who was older than she was. Wrinkled like an old tomato, wizened and bent over. I couldn't believe my eyes when I saw him 'cause he looked like a leprechaun, even though he was Scottish, with a twinkle in his eye and an accent to die for. A bag of tools held gently in his callused hands, but his hands had these long fingers that went on forever, delicate looking, and they seemed to move even when he was holding them still. They reminded me of old Chinese couples practising tai chi in the park of a morning, all smooth and slow, like moving through water.

Granny just pulled him in and set him going. He disappeared for a few hours, then reappeared like some sort of magician. No puff of smoke, no flash of light. Just now you don't see me, now you do. And he's there standing in front of me with a shitload of wood on his back and commences to build me a bed. It was just like magic, but not that bullshit David Copperfield "I'm a magician and I'm going to let the whole world know it." But a quiet, confident magic. A magic you can believe in. That makes you believe elves and pixies do exist. Granny called him Mr Bartholomew; nothing else, just that.

Check that my legs are creamed properly. I gotta be creaming my skin 24/7 'cause I must have the driest skin in the universe and there is nothing worse than seeing a black man walking down the street with white elbows, knees and ankles. Sorry-looking sight, and now that it's summer, that shit can't be done. Run my hand across my bald head and breathe deep. Step to my set and pull my spliff holder and lighter off my deck. Flip it open and pull out one of my readymades. I try not to let 'em stay in there for too long, a day or three at the most, otherwise they get dry and harsh and burn the fuck out of my throat. Light one up and sit back into my director's chair, the one with my name stencilled in on the back in big black marker. Blow out smoke and watch it spiral. I love watching smoke, watching it drift towards the ceiling. Taking up space, fogging a room until you can only see murky forms sliding through. But more than smoke I love the scent of weed, so sweet, so potent. Nostrils catching it, getting stoned on it and you're not even smoking, just sitting in the same room.

"Fuck."

Iago's leaning hard on his horn again. Shattering the silence of the evening. I hate when niggas be leaning on the horn instead of just taking their lazy selves up the stairs and knocking on a man's door.

"What do you want?"

I'm leaning out of my window, shouting down at him as he leans on his Mini as if he's some sort of Mac Daddy pimp from the nineties.

"You coming down?"

"I told you already not to be leaning on your horn."

"You ready?"

"Am I wearing my shirt? If I am, then I'm ready."

"Hurry up, I got to pick up Dean."

Look around for a second, disorientated. Grab my keys, my sunglasses and the most essential part of my ensemble: my spliff holder and lighter. Shove them into various pockets, then spend the next few seconds fishing out my sunglasses and putting them on. Got to look cool in the summertime. Pick up my records in their shiny silver boxes and heft 'em downstairs. Shove my head round Mum's door.

Mum's reading a book, some heavyweight text. She's always reading someone, Dostoevsky, James Joyce, Tolstoy, Dickens. Just full on, no sellout works. She's laid out on her bed, wearing some Russell Athletic sweats that I brought for her. The small reading glasses she wears perched on the end of her nose, a jug of her special brew homemade lemonade beside.

"Where are you going?"

"Playing out, it's Josephine's birthday."

"You be good now."

"Yeah, I'll see you later."

Iago's got the Mini turned around and is sitting on the bonnet. Iago's my best friend; we been together since we were twelve. Same class in school after I transferred. Me, Iago and Danny, the three musketeers. Iago's got four sisters, two older, two younger, and we've decided for friendship's sake that I'll be leaving them all alone. But I have to say that they are fine, fine as may wine. At times it's difficult indeed to just let them be. Which is one of the reasons I don't go round to Iago's as often as I should. Being in his house is enough to drive any man insane. With all the hollering and yelling, half-naked flirting with you.

First there's Esta, she's the oldest, twenty-six, went to school with Juli, she's just about to finish a degree in accounting, somewhere or another. Big hair, big laugh and looks that'll cut you in half. She's also got a hard tongue on her, which can lead to some nasty bruises on the ego.

Then there's Chandler, Iago's twin. She was born a minute or so before him. She works for Barclays. I told her to move to the co-operative bank because Barclays is the kind that'll stiff you. But like all the women in Iago's family, she's got a mind of her own. But she is fierce, just unremittingly hard. All sharp edges and places to get cut. I don't know why she's so hard; Iago ain't saying, Chandler ain't saying, so I'm left wondering.

Next is Vanessa, seventeen. Now she's deadly, and she wants me, which isn't good, not good at all. Doing her A-levels, she wants to be an architect or something. She told me that she was out for a man with a fast mouth and a devil-may-care attitude. Her words, I assure you.

Then there is Nola, thirteen. Youngest of the Styles clan and doing those teen things: posters, song lyrics, crushes. She's got that colt-like grace and awkwardness that comes with being unsure what your body is about to do next. But her mind's as sharp as all the others. Just cuts to the chase and takes you out if your shit is weak.

Iago, like the rest of his family, is tall and rangy; long, as my mum would say. Obviously no one stepped over him as a child. He's dark, as dark as I want to be, obsidian. He attracts light, his dark skin absorbing it. He's got these thin-ass eyebrows which are prone to being raised in disbelief, and eyelashes which his sisters constantly tease him about. His eyes are dark, prone to filling with tears or becoming grim with ill-concealed anger, and his nose has flaring nostrils which are emphasised by the big silver hoop which pierces the left one. His lips, soft and pouting, often curling into a slow smile, reveal white teeth that wouldn't be out of place in a Colgate commercial.

He's leaning on his pride and joy as I come towards him: his '66 Broadspeed GT. It's a Mini coupe which looks like a Mini hatchback, or if you're me, a duck. Alloy wheels, low-profile tyres, lowered suspension and a big fucking engine. Well, big for a Mini anyway; 1400cc fuel-injection and a five-speed gearbox. How he manages the insurance on it I will never know. Iago believes his car to be a jet fighter and drives it as such, pulling on his aviator glasses and doing his Tom Cruise impression.

"I feel the need, the need for speed."

He's been hauled over so many times it has become embarrassing. But sitting in it is like nothing on earth. Wherever we go, nothing, no other car, pulls as many stares. It might just be the fact that the sound emanating from the car is loud enough to destroy eardrums at sixty paces, but I personally believe it to be the all-round class of the car. It is just so strange and exciting, not like your Vitaras or Golf Cabriolets or BMWs that every other nigga drives. It just makes a statement straight out the box. Dark metallic blue it is. Don't ask me where he got it from, 'cause I don't know.

"You gonna give me a hand or pretend you're Huggy Bear?"

"Keep that pimp shit to yourself, I ain't wearing flares and platforms."

"But you got the Afro."

"This is my Black Panther, militant-nigga-on-the-real-deal Afro."

"If you say so."

"Just get your shit in the car."

"No, not shit. Records. R-E-C-O-R-D-S. Records are not shit, records are precious articles of our society, a chronicle of black life."

"Yeah, yeah, just get them in the car."

Look at him as he loads up the records onto the back seat and into what little space he calls a boot. His Afro rubbing the doorframe, he hasn't combed it for a few days and it's just standing up on his head. His sunglasses lost in a forest of hair. Dressed as casually as I in his Michigan basketball top with Chris Webber's number on it, dark Adidas shorts and his Reebok classics.

Jump into the car and slide myself into the movable racing seat from Recaro that folds forwards so others can get into the back. Iago adjusts his rearview mirror, kicks the car into gear and slides it dangerously out into the street. He flicks on his set using the little control column by his steering wheel and cranks up the volume. Now, for a man who purports to be a DJ, I find it strange that he doesn't have a set in his house. But no, he fills his car up with the darkest set known to mankind. People know we be out, because that driving bassline does come before us. The front of the car's a mess of tapes, some in cases, some not; some labelled, most not. Iago spends most of his time driving searching for a specific tape, which he never finds. Well, not while I'm in the car.

"Listen to this, I hooked up another bass bin."

A flick of a switch and I'm encased in sound like a strait jacket. The bass is enough to deafen mortal men, but we be niggas, so we just nod our heads and feel our hearts flutter at the bass's touch. Nod my head to "Buck 'em Down," the remix with the sung chorus.

Buck 'em down
buck 'em down, buck 'em down, buck 'em down
buck 'em down…

I sing along, then Iago comes in with his rich tone. I've never been able to carry a tune, so I always feel a pang of envy whenever anyone else can. Iago's sliding in and out of traffic, heading towards Dean's, an old school friend, one of the funkiest white boys alive, who's the living into jungle. Got his own little set-up in his room, sampler, keyboard, decks, Cubase system on this souped-up Mac and a whole load of extremely technical shit and wizardry which I should be into, but at this moment just can't get my head round. Iago stomps his foot hard on the brake and the seatbelt digs deep into my chest. He's cutting in and out of gaps I wouldn't even attempt on my bike. The engine revving, revving, revving. The back end shaking as he puts the power down. Hand gripping the short-shift gearstick like it's Daytona or something. No movement of the arm, all wrist. Slap, slap, slap. Fourth, back to second. Third hard into fourth, even harder into fifth, and flies are being sucked to their doom onto the windscreen.

My arm trailing out of the open window, dipping my hand into honeyed waters. Just trying to forget for a second the futility of this life. Born to die. Same shit, different day. If I believed in God I'd be screaming at him by now, asking, *Why is the world this way, why*? All I've got is my bike, my set, my records and Iago. I don't count family, Mum and Juli and Granny. Family's always there, they are just family. Love them or hate them, they are family, with you evermore. Friends are something else. You choose them and you can lose them. There are no special bonds that tie you to them. You choose to be friends, and that is the magic of it.

See the orange blobs float past from underneath closed lids and wonder why I'm so pessimistic. Life ain't nothing but bitches and riches. But who am I fooling? I ain't a rude boy, and I don't live in Compton, South Central L.A, the Bronx, Staten Island, Brooklyn or anywhere else in the States. Just me and South London. You ain't gonna catch me in no camo gear, I ain't part of Smif & Wessun or Mobb Deep. No cross colours, string vests or ripped jeans. I ain't called Buju Banton. Just Eder the boy from Brazil in his golden top in the wilds of South London.

Rub my eyes and stretch and try not to knock Iago in his head. Squint at the clock in the dash: it's half eight. Iago takes a corner hard, racing changes. Look out the side, see the river flashing past. The lights rippling reflectively across its surface. Balls of light, glowing luminously, hanging there. Streaming past, bleeding one into the other. I love the day, but the night is when I feel most at ease, most at peace. A subconscious thing about not being black enough, not being dark of skin. In the dark, pigmentation doesn't matter, everyone's black. I fear that within my soul I am not black enough, that's why I surround myself with so much blackness — Iago, my records, my attitude — to reinforce my own blackness in the face of those with nothing to prove. But nothing's ever that simple. What is? And I sit here in Iago's speed machine with my head feeling as if it's about to burst.

Iago brakes hard and we're at Dean's. Stopped in front of a tower block. Get out and travel up in the lift. I stop counting once we get past fourteen and just stare at the silver interior, not like the lifts on the circuit. You'd never find a lift that clean here. Step out on the twenty-fourth floor and walk down to Dean's door. From inside can be heard the deep sounds of some dark bassline, and I feel my head just nodding along with it.

Dean pulls open the door, a wave of smoke rolling over us as he stares out, a smile on his face and a spliff clamped between his lips. His long blond hair pulled back into a ponytail. He's decked out in some grey shorts, a green surgical vest and a pair of Timberlands that he's wearing without socks.

"Hey, how you two doing?"

We hug, first Iago then me. It's good to see Dean. I haven't seen him in a while. He kinda just drops off the face of the earth. When Dean isn't holed up in his yard making jungle tracks, he's an engineer in a studio in the West End somewhere. Helping some up-and-coming pop act remix its latest tune. We step inside and the beats just flying at you. He's got speakers hooked up everywhere. Surprisingly, it's light inside and tidy. Most people, upon seeing Dean, believe it's going to be a sty. We all tramp down to the nerve centre of this operation, the bedroom. Where all of Dean's fancy gizmos are kept.

"You ready, Dean? We ain't got much time."

"Yeah, I'm sorted, just got to get my jacket and some skins."

He potters around in his room for a second, pulling on a faded jean jacket and sliding a pack of Rizlas into his jacket pocket. He bends down and grabs his box of records, handing his spliff to Iago, who draws deep. Takes a quick look around.

"You got everything?"

"Shit, almost forgot."

Ducks over to his table and pulls out a tape, a nice metal tape that if I remember rightly costs a tenner a go in all good electrical stores. Waves it in front of his face as we walk out the door.

"You have got to listen to this."

Iago drives fast, it's like being on a rollercoaster, you don't know whether to scream or to cry. So instead you just hold on for grim death. After a while you get used to it, but the first couple of times it's really fucking scary. Now, if you're Dean and this is your first spin around with Iago for a long time, the way to get away from that feeling of fear is to be smoking pure weed spliffs. When he passes it forward and I take a toke of it, I can feel my head slowly disintegrating. Eveything's just slipping away, and I'm surprised by how quickly it's got to me.

Dean leans forward.

"You've got to listen to this."

I take the tape from his hand and slip it into the deck, Dean sits back and I turn and see him just smiling as an eerie wailing enters the car. The wailing goes on for what seems a long time before a very clipped beat steps into the arena with a demon sub-bass throbbing under it. Nod my head and start to hum the drumroll, which sounds like a variation on Apache. Then everything fades down and a Jimi Hendrix guitar break comes over the top, hard and forceful, then the living B-line just drives through and I look back at Dean, who's still got that Cheshire Cat–grin on his face.

"This is dark."

"Ain't it just."

"Let me be the first to congratulate you."

"Thanx."

Iago stops the tape and rewinds it so we can all listen to is again as we burn rubber down towards Gerald's. Gerald runs the pirate station that we play on occasionally. Another old school friend. He's got his station out on this estate in North London. We're loathe to go there, but sometimes these things have to be done. Dean's a regular 'cause he plays the living dark jungle set. That does tear shit up all the time. I used to go round to his a lot and listen to the new stuff that he had, dub plates, test pressings and the like. We would go round to these little shops in the back of nowhere and come back with some of the darkest shit I have ever heard and there would be like only forty or fifty copies that the guy who made it was just sending out to see what kind of feedback he would get. Just so underground and subversive. Like we were some sort of freedom fighters out to take back our country by any means necessary.

I puff deep on the weed and let it flow through me as Iago takes the tyres to the limits of adhesion. Iago's puffing hard as well. Like the weed demon that he is. Arm stretched straight, the killer J hanging out of his lips, attached as if by magic to his lower lip. Moving every time he pulls on it. Tilting 45 degrees upwards, the end glowing, as off-white vapour flows down his nostrils out into the atmosphere. Every time I try to do that shit, I start to cough like a novice. Look out the side and see the forest of tower blocks coming towards up. The lights dotted along their heights. A random scattering. The ground floors with their security lights flooding the doorways (or they would be if they were all working).

The interior road we turn onto is filled with speed bumps to stop joyriders and excitable commuters looking for a shortcut to work from mowing down innocent little kiddies as they play.

The young ones, the wild ones, are out. Picture the estate through their eyes. The expanse of it, the despair of it. No place to go, nowhere to run. So let's create our own fun, hang out, smoke, rebel. Rob a house, knock over a car, discover the joys of sex in a stairwell that people have been pissing in forever. Teen pregnancy. School ain't saying shit. Hate the teachers, classes are boring. I'm not going to get a fucking job anyway 'cause I'm black and I live in England. Sit on the dole for as long as I live, stay on the estates 'cause everyone I know is here. Being a mother makes you someone, something other than just another face in the crowd. Gives life meaning, makes you somebody instead of nothing. Sit out in the sun and talk, chat about where the parties are. She's sleeping with him. Need to get some weed, need to get some new clothes, need new trainers. House party, dress up, rub up, bump and grind.

Iago slides it to a halt, and they're out there lounging on the steps. A quick look, a stare, gaze turns away. Nothing to be afraid of. Whatcha got? How much back up? I watch them for a few beats as the engine dies and rumbles edgily into silence. Silence which presses heavy on you until sounds filter back and I can hear their voices, hushed and quiet for the second but willing to explode into a hurricane of sound at any second. The sound of TVs high above, volumes up. A bassline driving hard, voices raised, an argument. A dog sticks its head over a balcony and starts to bellow, saliva spilling into the air. Each bark cracking across the dark spaces like thunder. The wind shafting through the buildings, soft sounds echoing as the grass rustles and the old beat-up cars which just sit, but never move, creak.

Haul myself out of the car with Dean following close behind and head over to the youths. They can't be more than fifteen, sixteen on the outside. Cigarettes glowing ghetto red-hot. The soft flickering fluorescent light above them illuminating the backs of their heads. Graffiti, juvenile in the extreme, scrawled across its plastic casing, then along the walls. Wonder how come they've never been able to find any new names, how the same old ones keep coming back, year after year. They lounge across the doorway, leaning nonchalantly.

"You know which floor Gerald's on?"

They look at me for a second, just a fraction before they answer.

"Fourteenth, red door."

"Safe."

Turn and head back to the Mini where Dean's standing there with his case of records in one hand.

"Do you guys want to come up?"

Look at my watch. Getting close to half nine. Josephine will kill us if we're late. She's hired out equipment specially. One of her exes is doing the DJing until ten, then it's down to us. Doing it for free, but you know got to build up a good relationship.

"Nah, we gotta go. Tell Gerald we'll be seeing him around."

"Yeah."

Dean walks over to the door, puffing on his spliff. The boys look at him. He turns and waves at us before getting to the door. He hands one of the boys his spliff and carries on through while we pile into the car and Iago takes us out along the exit road.

Party Time

I slip the record out its sleeve and stare into its depths. The grooves within it. So much information held within it. Put it onto the turntable and move it back and forth. Fingers touching. Forefinger straight. It's as if I'm in a trance, the monitor echoes behind me, the sounds of the Alkaholiks around me.

First comes respect,
money comes next...

Bring the other record up to speed. Slip the volume up and match beats. Adjust the headphones that are on top of my head and move my neck a little to the right to get rid of the crick that's developing in it. I watch the label spin, a dark smudgy fingerprint rotating close to the edge, drawing my eye. Scratch slightly, cutting hard across the other song. Rhythmic, in time. Melding, creating a new form. Smile to myself as I let the vinyl go, as the songs fuse together. The two components becoming one in the crucible of the mix.

The sensation of concentration drifts slowly through me. I can feel myself sinking deeper into a trancelike state of mind. When it's just me and the music, the decks becoming an extension of me, just as my bike does when I ride. No need to think about what I'm doing, just go with the flow. Go with my gut instinct and make it happen. Just like a Nike ad. Just do it.

Iago taps me on the shoulder and I look round. He taps at his watch and I look down at mine, I've overrun my slot by a good twenty minutes. Smile and shrug. Iago knows me. When I get into the groove, it's a bastard getting me out. I hold up my finger for one more and he looks at me as if to say, That's what you said twenty minutes ago. Which is the truth. I did say it twenty minutes ago.

I turn back to my box, the sleeves turned on their sides sticking out of it, and put back the Alkaholiks, flicking through them to pull out "One More Chance." My tune of the moment. Spin back the other tune halfway through and let the intro roll in. Take a quick look up as the crowd's hands hit the air and the bodies sway.

First things first,
I poppa freaks all the honeys...

Take the headphones off and hand them to Iago, who slips them on.

"Get me a drink?"

"What?"

"Red Stripe."

"Sure you haven't had enough?"

"Two cans of Red Stripe don't put me over the limit."

Puts his arm around my shoulder and pulls me close as if to whisper in my ear before breathing heavily into my face. The hard, coarse smell of just-ingested beer streaming over my face, across my nostrils. I wrinkle my face up in disgust and push him away as he starts that witch's cackle that he calls a laugh. His laughter losing itself in the music as I head for the door.

People press against me, a seething mass. Hands in the air, heads nodding. Josephine always did know too many people. It's one of the byproducts of being a honey. Everyone wants to hang out with the beautiful people. The darkness of the room only alleviated by the diffused light coming from a covered window and the small lights that illuminate the turntable that seems so far off in the distance. Some of the niggas in the place are pushing their lighters into the air. Flaring, flashlight bright. Making sure they ain't stepping to no strobe-light honey.

I move slowly through the crush, turning sideways, arm extended, touching backs, feeling the curve of spines, the ribcages as I press gently and ease my way forward, nodding my head as Iago changes tracks.

Nothing but the dog in me,
a nothin,
a nothin but the dog in me...

Get to the edge of the crowd, by the door, and look back. It isn't that far to the decks, but it took the living time to get across the gap. Iago is revealed and concealed by the mass of dancers. Pull open the door and step out into the brightness, feeling as if I should reach into my pocket and pull out my shades. As my eyes make the transition from near total darkness to light. Stand blinking for a second before moving forwards through the thinner crowd of people out in the hallway. Most of them are chatting amongst themselves, whilst others hold up the walls. Drinks held in their hands, sipping from them occasionally. I look at them and I don't know whether they're together or flying solo. As I move, I get the living jolt in my abdomen and I recognise that I'm dying for a piss. Head upstairs, treading carefully to avoid stepping on the people sitting there, and find that there's a queue. Lean against the wall and look at my watch. Half three.

Iago moves into Brownstone, with Craig Mack with that old futuristic, robotic, George Jetson shit, throwing down his lyrics. Nod my head and feel the back of it tap gently against the wall. The queues moved a bit closer, but not much, and my bladder's squeezing tight and it's taking all of my attention to keep from leaving a puddle on Josephine's floor. I haven't pissed myself since I was fourteen and got tickled too much by Juli while watching *Knight Rider*. It wasn't my fault, she just leapt on me. Took advantage while I was having a weak moment as I watched David Hasselhoff's bouncing bouffant. She pulled out a sneak attack. Stealth sister coming in under my older sibling radar before dropping the bomb on me.

Take another quick look down the line and it's the same length. Hasn't moved at all. Head back downstairs and out the door. My eyes blind to all before me as I rush nonchalantly out the front door. Through the small knots of people sitting on cars that don't belong to them. Smoking. The glowing scarlet tips luminous in the dark, lighting their faces. Smoke pouring from flared nostrils. Their voices are hushed, strange; black people are usually so loud and forceful. To see us quiet is weird, almost unnatural. But I'm not waiting to see if maybe these are like horribly mutated black people. Like something out of *The X-files*. Some huge government cover-up.

I don't look back as I head off down the street, look up and down before pulling out my dick and pissing while I walk. The sensation is intense. The release beyond belief. As the fluid pours from me, splattering the pavement in front of me. Pissing while you walk is a technique best perfected when it's not windy. I whistle gently as I shake off the last dregs, putting my close friend away and heading back to the party.

I shift inside the house, not sparing a backward glance for those lounging outside. The passageway is fuller now, black people have appeared in force. It's as bad as when I left the front room. Twist my body to angle through, my fingers brushing thighs, breasts and butts, male and female. Keep my fingers relaxed, neutral. Trying not to step on anyone's feet or stare into anyone's face. People seem to take exception to this and screw bad when it happens. As if by looking at them you're throwing down a challenge. I try not to, but the urge is irresistible. I feel I have to look at people, see how their faces are put together. Study their features, one at a time. Look at them separately before putting them back together and seeing how the whole fits together. Whether I find it attractive. Whether the eyes being a fraction apart would make it better. The lips being fuller or wider. Less prominent cheekbones, a stronger chin.

I'm always examining, looking, observing. I don't know what I'm looking for. The idea of plastic surgery disgusts me, makes me go cold to think of someone changing my features. This is how I was born, who am I trying to kid by changing it? So then what does all this examining of peoples features mean? If I wouldn't change mine, why should someone else?

I drift and shift through the crush, looking for openings and gaps. My eyes flitting across faces. Looking at them for an instant before darting away and sliding across someone else's.

Feel a shove in my back and I'm thrown forward. Lurch into someone. Try to steady myself, but can't. The weight coming from behind is too much. a whole bunch of people move as one, shifting from one side of the passageway to the other.

"EHHHH!"
"HOL' UP!"
"MAKE WAY!"
"COMING TRU!"

"MIND OUT!"

"JESUS!"

Everyone's making up a whole heap of noise and I'm pressed into some girl's chest. At another time it would be extremely enjoyable, but right now it feels as if my spine's about to break.

"Sorry."

I mumble into her hair, can't even move my head to catch a glimpse of what's happening behind me. Move my feet to get a little purchase and start to think about pushing back when the pressure just comes off and I can stand normally again. Take a step back as the raised voices become murmurs of discontent at the brutal treatment they have just received. Look down on the girl I've been leaning on and apologise again. She's cute. Dark skin and a pair of gorgeous eyes. Her body's encased in a shiny red dress which stops at about mid-thigh. She looks up at me and I smile, my twisted crooked smile. She doesn't respond, just a flicker in her eyes, which turn away from mine. Shrug and move through the crowd towards Josephine in the kitchen.

"Fucking idiots!"

"This ain't carnival. Shit."

"Black people just don't know how to behave."

"Little youts."

Say hi as I pass by. Nodding and smiling to faces I vaguely remember and those I know closely. Edge through the hands holding plastic cups filled with Bacardi and Coke or some cheap white wine purchased from the local off-licence. Cans dripping with ice water tilted towards lips or held against thighs.

The kitchen has a table across the door, with Josephine's older sister Irene on guard duty. Her forehead is heavily creased and she doesn't look happy. It's the face of someone caught up in multiple quadratic equations, with no end in sight. I have to move my face in close to hers and leave it in front of her for a while before she sees me.

"Oh! Hi."

"Hi."

I reach out my hand and place it on her forehead and with my thumb start to knead away the stress that I see there. Place my other hand on the juncture of her neck and shoulder and lightly massage her there as well.

"Is that better?"

She just nods, her eyes closed. I continue for a minute or two until I see her visibly relax before I stop and give her my order.

"Eve always said you were good with your hands."

Smile and shrug.

"Can I have a can of Red Stripe?"

She moves over to get the drink while I lean on the table.

"Why so stressed?"

"Waiting for my results."

"For your degree?"

"Yeah."

I feel my heart lurch for a second and wonder why I amn't at university, getting a degree, making something of myself, rather than riding my bike around London trying not to get killed and playing out on the weekends. Irene comes back with the can and I lean across and kiss her on the cheek.

"What's that for?"

"I wanted to, is that a crime?"

"Do you always do what you want to?"

"Only where girls are involved. I'll see you later."

41

Make my way back through the crowd. Iago's playing Ol'
Dirty.

Oh baby I like it raw,
yeah baby I like it raw...

I sing along, making my voice dirty and rough, raise my hand
and swing my palm in time with my head. Love that song,
love that sound. Look inside the front room and it's just as ram
as before. I edge into the crowd and dance with everyone else.
Close my eyes and lose myself in the music. Nod my head and
swing my arms. Shuffle slightly. I'm straight out of the school
of minimalist dancing. Don't move too excessively, don't get
too sweaty. Just dance cool and smooth on the beat. Unless of
course it's jungle. Then a man's got to get sweaty and jump
up. But hip hop, swing, ragga, rare groove; the dance is the
same, just a little variation here and there, but virtually the
same. Move real smooth and don't take up too much space. I
don't take up much space, and I expect others to do the same.
Don't be shoving up against me like I'm a bitch. Keep your
distance, keep your elbows out of my face and your feet off
mine and we'll get along fine.

Niggas
grab your dicks if you love hip hop...

Twist and swirl, my head is low, nodding, so are my lids.
Blood-crimson glowing flares smoulder dully in my vision.
Stop abruptly as the record jumps, sharp scratch. The feeling
is lost as the beat jumps out of sync with us the audience. I
look up and see Iago staring daggers into the crowd, shaking
his head before lowering it and continuing to mix.

Get back into the music and let Biggie Smalls' verse flow. Laid-back East Coast anthem. I don't know what I would do without hip hop. More than that, what I would do without black music. My whole life, my whole outlook on life, my personality is predicated on black music.

Here's a revolutionary thought for you. Music should be free. You shouldn't have to pay for it. It's too important to be owned by the few, it should be readily available to the many. Music plays too big a part in people's lives. Whatever is not food, clothing or heating is a want, not a need. Music is a need, through music we construct definitions of ourselves, rebel, rejoice and articulate our deepest fears and desires. The ability of music to encapsulate a moment, a feeling, an emotion and transcend race and class is beyond measure. The ability to change a day from shite to glorious within four minutes is something that should be free to everyone.

Smile and shake my head at my meandering thoughts, then the record skips again and I stand frozen as Iago cuts out the sound and talks fierce.

"Listen you big-foot nigga, if you can't dance without bumping the table, then don't dance. You get me?"

I'm making my way through the crowd before he's finished, because Iago's got a temper on him that's volcanic, and once the lava starts flowing, there ain't no putting it back. Why do you think I keep well away from his sisters? Because if I were to do them wrong, I'd be on the wrong side of his temper. The crowd's silent, but I know they won't be silent for long. Someone starts to say something, but Iago slams up the volume and overrides the voice. He's muttering like an old crone when I get to him, his face all screwed up as he searches for a next record.

"What's going on?"

"Little fucker keeps bumping the table. Stares me dead in the eye every time like he's got something to prove."

"You know him?"

"I don't know him from Adam, but if he does it again he'll know my fist real well."

Look at the guy he pointed at. Some black youth who can't be more than eighteen and five foot five. Mean-looking little bastard, with his Stone Island puffer, too much gold, over a string vest and those oversize Karl Kani jeans. On top of his head he's got those nasty-looking Versace shades just above his forehead. I watch shorty as Iago pulls out a tune and starts to line it up as the crowd responds to the music that's playing. Shorty tries to grab a girl in a short black dress with straightened hair and a gold tooth. She looks at him and cuts her eye. I'm surprised I'm not seeing blood. Turns her back and creates some space between them. My boy doesn't look disappointed, just stands there for a second before acting as if nothing happened and trying to chirps a next woman. A lighted spliff appears in his hand and he blows smoke rings into the ceiling.

Scan the crowd and watch the motion, the sea of heads, a sea to lose yourself in. The great sea of rhythm when all are one.

Shorty slides around behind another girl, all up on her arse. Smiling wide. Leave him to it as Iago mixes in the next song. He's staring intently at the back of shorty's neck as he edges closer and closer to the decks. Suddenly I remember the can of Red Stripe dripping on my palm and hand it to him. Iago pops it open and takes a long chug, leans forward and belches softly in my ear.

I push him away as shorty bumps the table, and Iago's shouting like a nigga, lunging forward. I grab him and hold him back, turn him around, whilst shorty's standing on the other side pretending he's Chris Eubanks.

"Just stay with the decks, keep playing."

I've got no time for hard-faced niggas who be thinking they stateside. Fuck 'em. See his eyes looking at me. Going up and down, trying to see what I'm made of, how far he can push me. which buttons he should push. I don't even look him in the eye, just keep my head down and move into the space around him. The space that magically appears around any antagonists. The crowd parts and the space appears.

Step to him and place my mouth near his ear. Feel him tense as if I was going to drive my fist into his face. Violence has never been my forte, I've never been one for getting the shit kicked out of me. But when push comes to shove I gotcha back.

"Why don't you just move away from the decks and dance somewhere else?"

My boy kisses his teeth.

"Okay so you think you're a rude boy. Nice, nice. But if you keep bumping the decks I'm going to turn off the tunes and wait until you move. Then you can tell all these people why they ain't dancing."

Give him a second to think about it before I turn away and head for the decks. He's watching me, as is everyone else. I lean across the decks and pull down the volume to a whisper.

Silence dominates. It stretches taut and sharp like a rubber band between us. I let it sit there. Like a pregnant toad. All fat and bloated. It hangs and hangs and hangs and hangs. Each second an eternity within which universes could be created. The crowd stands waiting, their voices starting to rise. From low murmurs to discontented shouts. Soon they'll be throwing their plastic cups and their empty beer cans. Look over my shoulder and smile at shorty standing there by his lonesome. See the gears spinning in his head. What to do, what to say, what to be.

I want to believe it's my smile that breaks him, but I know it's the silence. Just the weight of it lying on his shoulders. Lying between shorty and the rest of the crowd. He moves, cutting back into the crowd. I breathe again and let the volume come back up. From the speakers Craig Mack breathes life back into the jam.

Here comes the brand new flava in your ear,
time for new flava in your ear...

I go back round to Iago and smile a little smile, but his gaze is off over where shorty disappeared.

"Let it go."

"Let what go?"

"He ain't worth it."

"Just give me a gun and I'd shoot him. Blow a hole in him."

"Did I tell you I used to have a list of people that I'd shoot if I had a gun?"

"Yeah, nigga'd be first in line on mine."

"I'd go down this list and think, Yeah, you'd be dead. One shot to the head. Or, Nah, I'd just shoot you in your kneecaps, let you suffer."

"Yeah, I'm with that."

"Just play your tunes."

"Hush your mouth."

"You know what they say."

"What?"

"Those that can, do; those that can't, play records."

That smile's back, and I'm glad. When Iago gets grim and dark, I'd rather be somewhere else. Last New Year's I thought he'd killed this guy outside a club, but he'd just knocked him unconscious. We had to carry him to hospital and stay with him in accident and emergency for over three hours while he was seen to. Said we were friends and my boy had gotten into a fight, gave false names then ducked out. Not one of the best New Years I've ever had.

There's a surge of people heading towards the decks just like a wave. Can't see what's going on, everyone's shouting and yelling. Arms in the air as they twist away from the centre of the storm. They hit the decks and I'm already leaning against it to stop the table from toppling over. Push hard. The needle pops out. And I'm praying that nothing breaks. Shouts, curses. It's too dark to see anything. Just hear the thuds and the yells. Breath being expelled, girls screaming and general mayhem. The sheet over the window is ripped away with a loud crack and moonlight pours in. Silhouetted against the light, a circle has formed around a heaving mass of bodies. Can't tell whether it's two, three or four people. Just that there's a struggle going on. The door bursts open and people stream out, while others are trying to get in. Tungsten glare as the light switch is flicked. The silhouette's gain form and substance.

Shorty's kicking shit out of some youth whilst being dragged off by a whole group of niggas. Flash of silver in his hand and he's waving it like a nutter. Knife, can't tell what sort. I ain't moving. See Josephine struggling through the exodus of people.

The knife cuts, a hand is drawn away and clutched close. See that red rush pump over the fingers clamped tight around it. Shorty's free and looking for another target, since my boy's lying on the floor.

Iago hits him in the side and takes him to the wall. There's just a blur. Just a whirl of sound and fury. All I can see as I fight my way through the hovering, voyeuristic crowd is just a confusion of limbs and action. Push Josephine out of my way as I get to the space.

Iago's standing over shorty, who's lying prone on the ground beneath a dent in the window frame the exact shape of his forehead. The knife is still clutched in his hand.

"Somebody phone the police."

Aftermath

We haven't said anything about the party. My shoulder's still wet from Josephine's tears. All she wanted was a party, a good party that everyone could enjoy themselves at. To be able to revel in this summer radiance that is all too soon gone. I don't know whether Iago wants to talk about it or not, but I have to. You learn that sort of thing in counselling, it's best to get it out right there and then and as many times as you need to. Rather than letting it fester inside you and corrupt your soul. Making you bitter and twisted. I hate to see black people like that. All that senseless posturing and machismo. Makes me ashamed to be black sometimes.

"Why do nigga's do it? What do they have to prove?"

"They ain't got shit, so they gotta have something to define themselves against."

"We all black, what's there to define? We all in the same situation. But we don't have to fight and die over someone scuffing our trainers."

"Maybe we're a bit more intelligent than they are."

"Bollocks!"

"The more educated you get, the further away from them you get."

"Who's them?"

"Everyday nigga, that don't question the situation, that don't want to do nothing except exist from day to day. More worried about getting those Versace shades than looking after their child."

"But are we that different?"

"If we're questioning it, of course we are. And anyway you're pale like a motherfucker."

"What difference does that make?"

"It means you closer to white, and niggas curse you for it."

"What's my skin colour got to do with niggas acting dark?"

"Too much energy and nowhere for it to go. Persecution, oppression, racism. You can't get away from it, and skin colour is the embodiment of that oppression. Makes them see what they can never have, so they say, Well alright, fuck all y'all."

"But that don't mean you got to fuck over black people."

"Who else you gonna fuck over. Only black people understand black people."

"Why carry on so stink for? What do they have to prove?"

"But you know what burns me the most is that sistas be jumping on roughneck who two-time, get 'em pregnant and then duck out."

"Then they be coming looking for a nice black man, but by that time, they already got a kid and man ain't having that."

"Black women carry on stink."

"Ain't that the truth."

We ride in silence as the lights slip past us. A constant flicker on our faces as we rush beneath them.

"What are we afraid of?"

"Us or black people in general?"

"Black people."

"We're afraid of being outsiders, of being driven out from the tribe. Of not matching up to some mythical pattern of blackness, which no one has ever written down, because it's just common sense. And which no one understands but that everyone accepts."

"Fear of becoming a sell-out."

"Yeah, so then education becomes something you want to avoid, because it's associated with white people, the white establishment, and if you associate yourself with white people you become white. So we gotta keep it real, keep it black."

"Do you think of me as black or white?"

"I think of you as you. Eder O'niah. We're friends, but that doesn't mean I don't see that your skin's lighter, your hair's curlier and your eyes draw the girls like flies. But I know you're black, everything about you screams, I'm black. From the way that you dress, to the way that talk, to the way that you think."

"I think of myself as black, but Juli was telling me that there were times at uni when she felt more comfortable with white people because she didn't have to be constantly proving her blackness. It was just taken for granted, you know? Their attitude towards her was that she was black, end of story. But then there'd be times when she would be with a group of black people and she'd feel insecure and that she's got to keep proving her blackness. But that no matter how hard she tries it's never enough. The girls all look down on her 'cause she's lighter and they want to be lighter, and the guys lust after her 'cause they just want light women, 'cause that's what society says is desirable. Now, I'm darker than Juli and I feel that sometimes. Like I'm not good enough, my skin ain't dark enough. The way that I am isn't black enough. I feel as if I'm trying too hard, and still not getting any closer."

I finish and we sit in silence as Iago keeps on trucking down the Chelsea embankment, heading for Battersea bridge.

I look in on Mum, even though it's well past five. But it's become a ritual. She has this habit of falling asleep with the TV on. Now she relies on me to come in and turn it off. Her glasses are still on and her book is open beside her. I creep in and put the book to one side, putting the bookmark back inside it, and gently take off her glasses. She moves in her sleep and mumbles something but doesn't wake and I quietly exit.

Step over my records to get to the kitchen. I don't need to turn on the lights, 'cause it's getting light outside. Look in the fridge for something sweet within its sterile white interior. Pull out two pots of yoghourt, grab a spoon from the plate rack and start stripping as soon as my door swings closed behind me. Pull my boxers out of my crack and sit on the edge of my bed. Peel the lid off the yoghourt and lick it clean before chucking it onto the bin that overflows with rubbish. Watch it carefully settle onto the top of the pile.

As I eat, I watch my reflection in the window. The light chocolate coloured skin and those damn eyes. A light green-brown. The same colour as Juli's, but with her they're the perfect complement to her olive skin. On me they look like an aberration. People always say there's something strange about me that they can't quite put their finger on, then they say it's my eyes, and I cringe. My straight nose with the flaring nostrils, it's not wide enough in my opinion but it gets me by, with my lips being as full as they are. My hair is usually curly, tight curls that if I leave long enough without washing turn into a jagged mess.

Shiver gently as cool winds blow through my window, get up and drag my records into my room. Flip open the top and hunt through until I find the record I want. Pull out D'Angelo and slip it onto my deck. Let that Prince-like sound waft through my head. Turn the bass up and lower the volume, letting the music fill my room. Finish the first yoghourt then dive into the second one. I ain't got no time to be collapsing on circuit just because I don't eat well enough. Crumple up the containers and chuck them at the bin. Watch as they land and then slowly slide away as the mountain of rubbish goes with it.

I hum gently under my breath, slow nod, eyes half closed. D'Angelo doing his thing about the girl, Brown Sugar.

Visions of chocolate-skinned beauties pass before my eyes. Thighs opening slowly underneath my fingers. Reflected in my nails, her face, eyes closed, lips parted.

I want some dark brown sugar
OOOOOOOOUUUHHHHHHHHH!

I've found whenever I see a girl I like, the words come unbidden, I start to sing in my off-key voice and smile a little smile at her to see whether she gets what I'm singing about.

I want to kiss a woman, touch her lips with mine. Just touch them very gently, very gently. Butterfly soft and run my tongue around the outline. Delve into that bow at the top.

I have a desire to touch and be touched. I love all tactile sensations, but especially skin touching on skin. Mum tells me how, when I was a baby, I would keep touching and touching and touching things. It didn't matter who held me, I wasn't picky, just as long as I could touch another person. Hold myself close to them. Juli at the same age would pull away from people and head for the floor, where she could explore and travel, whereas me, I'd sit on peoples laps and try to eat their necks.

Lean back and lay my arm across my eyes. Lie here breathing lightly. Little fingers of light edging under my closed lids. I have this problem; I sleep with my eyes open. Not totally open, just enough for it to scare every girlfriend

I've ever had. Comes from watching TV late into the night. Not caring what it was that was showing just not wanting to let go of my precious TV and the visual world of delights it offered.

So I stayed up late and bunked off school. Coming home straight after Mum left to catch some extra sleep before hanging out with the guys. Standing outside tube stations, meat markets, looking for girls, playing the arcades that were dotted around in kebab shops and taxicab offices. The only thing that kept me in school was Mr Maguire. Big white bloke. Scottish. He was huge, at least sixteen stone. We used to call him the walrus because he was just so fucking big. He had this curly handlebar moustache that hung from his upper lip like some sort of bedraggled rat. And when he spoke, you could hardly understand a word he said. With that thick Scottish accent and his machine-gun cadence. He was from Glasgow and you knew innately that he was hard, not just because of his size, but by the way he held himself. You knew he'd been through the wars and nothing we could do was going to faze him.

Up until I met Mr Maguire I'd been a hip hop head, still am. Big Daddy Kane, Eric B and Rakim, Run DMC, Biz Markie, Ultramagnetic, Juice Crew; you know, the Old Skool. I'd listen to them on the radio, making tapes, listening to Capital or the pirates, Kiss and LWR. Mr Maguire got me into jazz funk, rare groove. He brought in a whole load of records and just played them. James Brown, Funkadelic, Ohio Players, Blackbyrds, Meters. Just pure, old, sweaty funk. We sat there, with our heads going, recognising beats and breaks. After that Mr Maguire had new standing amongst us. People would die to get into one of his music lessons. The amount of people he signed up to learn to play instruments was just amazing. After a year of his being there we had a jazz quartet and a funk instrumental five-piece. It was just dark.

Listening to those '33s go round on his set, that he'd brought in with him in his beaten-up old Mark-2 Escort. We'd sit in wonder at the pureness of the sound. So clear. Everything was all there. The bass, the treble, but there was more of it, there was a greater clarity and depth than any of us had ever heard. It put the little set my Mum had to shame. I'd be buying records without a thing to play them on. I'd just look at the covers and save my shekels. Pouring over hi-fi magazines, speaking to Mr Maguire about what I should get, trying to figure out how I wanted it to sound. I'd get Juli to take me to hi-fi stores so I could audition different separates and listen to my precious records for the first time. Walk in there with my records tight to my chest, drooling at all the polished-silver finishes. Then Juli would drag me out after I'd been sitting in there for a few hours. Eyes closed, head nodding, basking in the glory of it.

Demon Run

I've found that I no longer need an alarm clock to wake me up, my body's got into that groove where every morning without fail I'll wake up at 7:30, no matter how hard I've been partying the night before. I might wake up at half seven and then go back to sleep until twelve, but I will always wake up at that time. Which is a comforting thought every now and then.

My lids roll open and already the light's igniting my irises. Roll over and out of bed and sit on the edge rubbing my face and groaning. A morning ritual from the years when I had to force myself to go to school on a cold winter's morning, with Mum hammering on the door and screaming at the top of her lungs for me to get my lazy self out of bed and out to school. Stand and stretch, getting the little kinks out of my back, then head for my decks. Stand for a second trying to decide which one to play, which one to play, a difficult decision at the best of times when you've got over two thousand records which you've been buying since the dawn of time. It's not only difficult because of the quantity, but also because you have to find the right song to match your mood. Got to scan through the memory banks until you figure out which one suits you before the mood slips away from you like spit down a drain. But after saying to yourself, Yeah, I want to listen to that one, then you've got to find it. Which isn't easy unless you're extremely anally retentive and have every record sorted, catalogued and with a little sticker on it saying how much it cost and where you brought it from, including dates and times.

I pull out Tuff Crew and slip it on. I feel like thinking about my not-so-innocent youth, reminiscing about the good old days. Like the Wu Tang say, "Everybody talking about the good old days, the good old days". Soup up the volume and head into the bathroom. I can feel the bassline follow me as I enter the shower, peel off my boxers and let the boiling-hot water sluice over me.

I sing the chorus, but the rest of the song I just mumble incoherently as the lyrics blur into strange fantastical words that make no sense if uttered to anyone listening close by, but which to me seem to mirror exactly the words I'm listening to.

I don't stay in the shower long, just enough to soap and spray and get myself ready. By the time I'm out, Mum's already been into my room and turned down the music. I turn it back up and start to cream myself, running the cocoa butter quickly across my skin, before spraying two deodorants under my arm pits and pulling on my work clothes. Look in my drawer and pull out a pair of brightly coloured boxers. Every girlfriend I've ever had who has seen my underwear believes my mother buys them for me. She used to, but she stopped that when I started making my own money. These girls seem to think that because I wear boxers with the Smurfs on, or bunny rabbits, my mum must have brought them for me, when I've taken a lot of time and trouble to pick them out myself. I can't wear some grey pair of boxers with a white strap across the waist that's got someone's name on it. Over these I pull on my cycling shorts, padded around the butt and groin to prevent saddle sores, and let me tell you, you don't want to get saddle sores, not ever. The cycling shorts are long, Endura down to just above my knees. Over these I pull on my Jordans. Black shorts with red trim and the Jordan logo flying across them. I wear these to protect my sense of self, my need to deny I have any homosexual urgings, and to stop too many men looking at my knob and my arse. If the world was full of women I wouldn't wear them, but since it ain't, they gots to be worn. Pull on a cycling top, choosing between either a long sleeve or a short sleeve. It's summer. I chose the short sleeve. The top has the logo of the courier company that I work for plastered over it, a circle pierced by an arrow, with the words Arrowhead International underneath. This logo is also on the Timbuk2 bag all the guys at the firm use, which you buy from the company for half the price you would get them for in the shops. And you know man has to have the best equipment going.

Pull on my specialized ground control over my socks and slip my lock over my shoulder, grabbing my Michigan cap and my specialized riding gloves as I head out the door. My shoes make no sound at all, the metal of the spd encased in soft carpet, but once I get onto the hard floor panelling in the kitchen it's another matter, with scratching following me as I walk around trying to get something to eat.

Wolf down a bowl of Weetabix and then make a few slices of toast, which I'm eating as Mum slides past me pulling on her coat and struggling with her bag and a cup of espresso. Mum's a coffee junkie, none of that soft Nescafe stuff, just full-on Italian espresso, small, sharp doses of caffeine intensity.

"Take care out on those streets, I don't want to be coming looking for you in hospital."Mum's warning is in my ear as she kisses me quickly on the cheek and heads out the door, the little cup of espresso sitting precariously on the shelf by the coat rack. She's already been to the hospital for me four times. I've broken my collarbone twice, fucked my knee and been seriously concussed all within the space of three hard years out on the circuit. Mum worries but she knows there is nothing that she can do to stop me from riding the circuit, it's what I want to do. So she contents herself with telling me to look after myself and to try not to get myself killed whilst I'm dicing with traffic. Pull out some juice from the fridge and pour it into my two water bottles, which I leave sitting on the table as I get myself all warmed up and stretched out. I never used to stretch before I rode, but when I pulled my hamstring, it was like, Nah, can't be doing this to myself. If I'm going to do this courier thing, I've got to do it properly, no half-stepping. So now I stretch before I ride, get my muscles working well and then ride like a nutter.

The only thing my mum really curses me about is the fact that I don't wear a helmet. There is no particular reason why I don't wear a helmet, I know I should, but I just don't. To justify myself in arguments with those stupid bastards that ask you this sort of question, I usually say helmets are damn fucking ugly, they're uncomfortable, they make you head sweat like fuck and finally, they engender this feeling of overconfidence that nothing can hurt you because you've got your helmet on and you're not going to die. If I don't wear a helmet I know that any chances I take will be taken on the odds of that particular moment in time rather than a false feeling of security. But you say this to someone and they just get a blank look on their faces as if you're trying to explain quantum mechanics or some other arcane art of mystic proportions.

I'm blowing slightly from the stretching that I've been doing. I bend down and swing my bag onto my shoulder, find that the strap of the bag is over my lock and put it back down, take off my lock and put it around my waist and then swing my bag over my head and across my shoulders, tighten the strap and pull my gloves over my fingers. I'm girding my loins for battle, my breath comes a little faster, my heart seems to be beating just a bit faster. Slip my walkie-talkie out of its charger, turn it on and slip it through the two pink pump straps that adorn my bag. Check I've got everything, money pouch, spliff case, lighter, Oakleys, keys. Yeah, everything's in check.

Turn and there she is lined up against the wall in all her glory. Light spilling across her and glinting off her black frame. A 1992 Kona Explosif, a seventeen-inch frame and a beauty at that. All steel and rubber. She's not as bright as she used to be, her colours a bit faded and I've let dirt start to collect on her, I'll have to clean her on the weekend. But sometimes you've got to let your bike go like that, so that she doesn't have that brand new, shiny, just-out-of-the-box, come-and-steal-me look. My bike loves me and I love it. I brought her just over six months ago and she hasn't given me a problem, not once.

I had to do a little tinkering on her, she wasn't as I would have liked, but what is? I had to change the front ring from a forty-six to a fifty, put an 11-19 road cassette on the back, change the rear derailleur for a road one. Put on a Ringle stem and change the headset. Put in a new titanium seat post, 'cause the old one was fucked, and put my old Vetta seat on it. Took off the knobblies that the guy I was buying it from had on it and put on some Conti Top Touring. Oh yeah, I also changed his bar ends to some X-lite stubbies.

If I told someone who has no interest in bikes whatsoever, they would have keeled over and died with boredom by now, but you tell that to another courier and they know. Their eyes light up and you can see the mind inside the head catching on fire at the thought of what he should do with his bike, what adjustments he can make, how he can tweak it just a little more.

I wheel her out of the door, pushing her along by her seat. Greer curses me for doing that, says I'm just acting flash and that she wobbles all over the place, that I should push her along from the handlebars. To this I give the finger and carry on in my own stubborn way. Lift her up and heft her onto my shoulder as I walk down the several flights of stairs before I get down to terra firma. Look at my watch: ten to eight.

"One one, one one."

Listen to the slight hum coming from my radio and wait for the reply. Hear Peter's slow drawl come down the line.

"One one, one one. Good morning, good morning."

"One one, one one back in the saddle, roger."

"Roger roge."

I call in before eight so that I don't have to work until eight in the evening. I hate working late. The system at Arrowhead is simple: you work a ten-hour shift. If you call in before eight, you work until six; before nine, until seven; before ten, until eight. But it's in my contract that if there's still work available I have to do lates, which I don't like, but I have done. At the end of the day it's more money in my pocket.

Step over the frame and slip my foot into the Ritchey spd's, hear the click and feel the meld come over me before I push off, bunny hop the curb and duck out into the street. Push myself up from the low-crouched racing position that my body bends into as I ride and lean back, pulling my Oakleys out of one of the two pockets at the back of my top and sliding them onto my face. My arms hanging limply by my side, swaying with my movements as I ride no-handed down to the junction.

It takes a strange combination of person to ride bikes for a living, to be a courier. I don't really know when I decided that couriering was for me, I just sort of slid into it. I suppose it's that addictive quality about me, that addictive quality about all working bike riders, in that there are so many bikes and so many parts, so many bits and pieces. For me, it was a natural progression from being obsessed with records and sound to riding bikes and getting a bike set up perfectly for me. A bike needs constant attention, like a dying aunt always calling you away from something that needs your attention just as urgently over something trivial. A brake block that is rubbing and squeals like some sort of warning device to pedestrians, a brake lever that's a little loose, a slightly buckled rim, a pedal that floats too much, a clunking in your bottom bracket. So many things that demand your attention, and if you're riding 24/7 it's twice as bad, because everything needs to be perfect for that peace of mind so that you're not worried. You're riding hard and taking risks, but you don't mind because you know the bike is set up alright and that it won't fail you. That's what you're paying upwards of five hundred notes for.

Swivel my head as a particularly luscious babe walks down the street, watch the perfect motion of her arse beneath the tight long skirt, let my eyes travel to her ankles and the black heeled shoes which move swiftly beneath her. Let out a long, low whistle and turn my attention back to riding. Swoop down and attach my hands to my handlebars, fingers meshing around the grip, two fingers out over my brake levers. Look right and turn left, heeling the bike over to the left, getting that angle between myself and the ground, inside leg bent to keep my pedal from scrapping concrete. Then I'm into traffic heading towards Vauxhall bridge. There's a massive tailback, they must be doing some sort of construction work on it or something, or some commuter's taken a cyclist to the kerb. Look to the inside of the queue of traffic and see there's no point going down there, so I switch to the outside, slice inside two cars and push the gear round as I pass cars and watch the oncoming traffic ease over to cut me some slack. She's moving slick and smooth, no noise coming from anywhere, except my breath loud in my ears over the soft clicking of the chain going round.

Riding with spds, it feels as if you are part of the bike, melded to it, that you and the bike are one, the only way that you and your bike could be closer is if you could have sex with it. That is how close you feel when you're attached by your spds. Look to the inside and see the commuters on their Treks and their Marins. The big rucksack perched precariously on their shoulders. Their wide bodies swaying as they spin around in a small gear on their compact drives. Their knees up by their shoulders because they haven't adjusted the seat to their height or changed anything whatsoever since they brought the bike. Look further up the road and see the commuters that think they're dons, who think that their Miguel Indurain or John Tomac. Decked out in all the gear, the pants the tops, the shoes, riding on their GT Zaskars or Cannondale Killer Vs. Trying to boot speed because they think they've got it, when they ain't got shit except a half-hour ride into and out of work every day. And because of that little ride they think they can tess. Try and race you when you've got the living packages on board, then when they can't keep up, try and draught you all the way to their destination. I hate commuters almost as much as I hate pedestrians, and only a little less than I hate all people in motor vehicles. I hate them because all of the above have no respect whatsoever for my safety, and if they have the opportunity they'll take me to the kerb without even knowing it.

What I fear most when riding is ignorance, those people who are so ignorant that they have no idea of the consequences of their actions and who in being so ignorant could cause me to die.

I arrive into Soho Square in a hurry. Some commuter tried to tess and I had to take him out going around Trafalgar square. Boot out into traffic and let him get swallowed up by the taxis. That's the way you tell the men from the boys, how they deal with traffic. You've only got a split second to decide, whether you dive through the gap or not, go to the inside or outside, slow down or jump the kerb. That's what I love about couriering, gutting it through traffic like a nigga, going into traffic with someone then finding that you've lost them when you get out. Wheel my bike up the steps and decide where I want to sit. The groundskeeper has his petrol-powered blower strapped to his back and is blowing leaves and old cigarette packets around the square, the engine on his back bellowing out a banshee wail. Nod at a few other couriers dotted around the place sitting on the benches because this time in the morning is about the only time when a courier has the opportunity to sit down on the benches.

I sit on a bench which is being peppered with sunlight and look at my watch. Just a little after eight, not too bad considering I didn't really have my foot down. Lean my bike up against the head of the bench and pull my bag over my head, setting it beside my feet. Pull a bottle out of its cage and take a quick swig, not too much otherwise I get a bit heavy in the morning and it's not conducive to riding fast.

"One one, one one."

"One one, one one."

"One one, one one, Soho square, roger."

"Roger roge."

Let Peter know where I am, otherwise he'll give all my

jobs to someone else. I'm lying, Peter's really good about that. He's the best controller I've ever had. And I know for a fact that I couldn't deal with sitting in a box all day telling riders where to go. Not after being a rider, I'd want to stay out on circuit forever, and once my knees were fucked from riding pushbikes I'd get a Ducati 916 and deliver packages on that.

Arrowhead's really different from other courier companies in that it only uses pushbikes. No motorbikes, no vans, just us couriers. That's how Peter likes it and wants it. He started the company about six years ago, brought it out from the company that he was working for, and has just kept it going and going. Most of the guys that ride for him are ex-Metro or SD. Peter wants only the best.

In my time I've worked for a whole load of companies, some good, most bad, and if I haven't worked there, I know several people who have. The first place was this company in Vauxhall, I don't know what their name is, they keep changing it so that people think it's a new company when it's just the same old company with a different name. That was when I had my big old muddy fox. That company was a bastard, I was with them for over a month during the holidays. They wouldn't give out walkie-talkies to new cyclists, they'd keep them for their motorbikes, and all of us pushbikes would lay our bikes outside and sit inside in a queue waiting for the next job to be given out, then ride to get the package, drop it off and then head back to the office. I was making about forty, maybe fifty a week, doing drops to North London, East London, a hell of places. Killing myself for this shitty fucking wage. At that time I was fifteen, so it seemed like I was making dollars, but after the first few weeks the shine of the money started to wear off and I was wondering, What am I doing this for? I might as well go and work in Sainsbury's. It wasn't until

I started chatting to other couriers that I figured out what a raw fucking deal I was getting, so I kicked that to the kerb and moved on.

The sun's moving higher, and the heat's coming like it's been coming for the past few weeks. Since the middle of June it's felt as if the whole of London was going to go up in a ball of flame. If this is the result of the ozone layer being destroyed, lets burn some more. The heat is hot, dominating everything, it weighs down on you, won't let you get up from under its influence. But I love it, turn my face to it and wonder religiously every night whether I have got any darker since that morning.

Take another sip from my bottle and let my head swivel, watching the Soho babes glide past, all at work in the media industry, their clothes telling where their fate lies. The old-skool Gazelles, the tight jeans, the leather loafers. the way that they walk, strut, preen. The people who haunt Soho believe they tell you what to wear, what to say, where to go. They believe absolutely that they influence you every day of your life. I watch them and I assess them and I wonder whether this is so. How affected am I by *The Face*, *i-D*, *GQ* and all the other magazines and style programmes and radio shows that say this is hip, this is now, get on this train or give back that fashion card you thought you had for life. I sit and I wonder, because as much as I deny it, I want to be a part of that glamorous exciting world. I want the beautiful women, the cars, the money, the adulation from people who know you not but want to be like you. Call it a weakness in my character, maybe that's why I became a DJ, because I wanted people to desire to be like me. That through music I would be able to influence others, to change perceptions, to control the way people interact with the world. I watch them, I think that maybe I've always been a voyeur at heart, an outsider looking in on a world that I desperately want to be a part of. Maybe it's what you get for being mixed race. And when you say mixed race, say it in an Afrikaans's accent. Mixed race. Roll that R.

"One one, one one."

"One one, one one."

"ADT Bloomsbury Square going W2, Manitou Frith Street going W3 and Timeless Golden Square going W1."

"Roger roge."

"Roger."

I'm leaning over my little plastic binder, scribbling the names of the pickups onto my sheet. Teeth working at the inside of my lip as I spin the names in my head. Wonder whether it's going to be a good summer. It usually gets a bit slow at this time of year with the influx of part-time summer riders flooding the circuits, taking money out of us year-round professionals' pockets. But Peter usually keeps the ball rolling. Him and Marilyn seem to find new accounts from out of thin air, and seeing as how he's already got a thick client base already, the riders on circuit shouldn't find that there's too much of a drop-off.

Get on my bike and cycle slowly out.

"No riding in here."

I don't even bother looking at the groundsman as I limbo under the bar, my bollocks brushing my top tube, and pull out into the West End traffic. I'm out of the saddle and riding hard, turning the gear round and checking around me. Dive through a closing gap and off down onto Frith Street. Pull a hard skid outside the office and grab a lamp post to chain my bike to. Then it's inside to my daily confrontation with the people who think that couriers are the lowest of the low. Secretaries and security guards.

"Hello?"

"Courier come to collect a package going to W3."

"Okay, fourth floor."

Lean back and pull open the door as the buzzer sounds. Press the button and wait for the lift to make its way down. I might be fit but I'm not walking up every flight of steps I come to, I'm taking the lift and if anyone's got anything to say about that they can suck my big toe. The lift is small, able to fit about two, maybe three people in at a time, and like most of the lifts I've encountered — and I've been in a few — it's mirrored. An infinity of reflections moving off to some far-distant vanishing point. No wonder everyone in the West End is so vain, they're constantly looking at themselves in their lifts.

Lift stops. Bowl down the corridor, my shoes squeaking on the shiny floor. Through the double doors and into reception, up to the desk. Look down on the big brown envelope. Look for the post code, check it's got a full address, scoop it up and head out without a backward glance. Totally disregarding the receptionist who's deep in conversation on the phone. She waves her hand in the general direction of the parcel before dismissing me from her consciousness. Decide to take the stairs down and romp happily down them, feeling the cold breeze of the air conditioning ruffle across my neck, and then down and out into sunshine and heat. The noise and the bustle of the city surrounding me.

I know the address the package is going, so I don't need to check in my AtoZ, which all couriers carry, don't let 'em tell you different. Because there are some addresses that even God can't find without the use of an AtoZ. Unlock my bike and head off for the other packages, swinging through traffic, it's early morning so it's not too heavy, but you can see it getting that way. Turn into a one-way street the wrong way and let the back end go in a skid as I come to a halt by the kerb. I carry my bike in through the security doors and leave it inside as I go up the one flight of stairs, and into reception.

"You look better every time I see you."

Louise is on the desk, a rather attractive blonde girl with heavy pendulous breasts that heave and shift under the tight tops that she wears. Her lips are an off shade of scarlet and her eyes are dark and heavily outlined.

"What do you want, flirt?"

"You know me, come to collect a package."

"I thought you were supposed to be taking me out to dinner."

"Oh yeah, dinner. When do you want to go?"

"What, you mean you're really going to take me this time?"

"Would I lie to you, Lou?"

I bat my eyes and turn my head slightly and watch as she starts to laugh. I grab the package and jet.

"See you later, we'll arrange a time and a place."

"You'd better."

When I ride hard I slip into a place deep within me from which I'm able to look out and see the road and a tiny strip around the road, but nothing else. That is the totality of my existence, and within that I am God and I am as fast as the speed of light. No pain is enough to stop me from gaining my goal, no rider is faster than me, and no motor vehicle is beyond my grasp. When my breath burns in my throat and my thighs are dying. Just dying. When my chest feels as if it is going to collapse. I ride harder. To ride hard you have to be a masochist. You have to be able to hurt yourself day in and day out, for two pound fifty a drop. You have to hurt yourself and in the hurting be reborn as if a phoenix. To slip into the zone when every movement is easy and feels as if it's being done without effort and you feel as if you could ride that way for ever. Just ride forever and ever and ever.

In space, if you push something somewhere it will carry on going that way forever or until it gets pulled into something's gravitational pull. That's what it feels like in the zone. Nothing can touch, change or transmute the pureness of the physical expression that you have reached.

Just like the feeling after a good fuck, actually.

I haul up outside a big building, lots of marble and shiny metal, lean my bike against the wall and bend to lock it.

"Can't leave your bike there, son, that's far too expensive."

I turn slowly and see some old security guard, balding, his white hair receding quickly into the distance, his face red and flushed. A gut hanging over his black trousers.

"'Scuse me."

"You heard me. Move your bike. You can put it over there."

He points towards some railings on the other side of the street. Stand up to my full height, push out my chest and stare at him.

"Can I bring it in then?"

"No, bikes aren't allowed in the building."

"I've been here before and I've locked-up here."

"Well not when I've been on duty."

I look at him. Timeless is on the fourth floor, don't want to carry my bike up four flights of steps, but I'm not about to go across the street and lock it up. He's got that security guard look down his nose at you, you're-shit attitude. So I heft my bike onto my shoulder and brush past him.

"Where do you think you're going?"

"To collect a package. Don't worry my bike won't even touch the floor."

Cyclocross it up the stairs with the guard huffing and puffing behind me, a flight behind. Push through the doors into the reception, being very careful not to scratch anything. Peter's going to have a fit when he hears about this. The receptionist is looking at me as if I'm naked before her, masturbating, as I come in to get the package.

"I've come to collect a package going W1."

She is still staring, so I repeat it again slowly for her.

"I've-come-to-col-lect-a-pack-age-go-ing-to-West-One."

"Oh yes."

She bends and pulls out a large brown envelope from around by her knees and hands it over. I take it in my hand, let it hang between us for a second longer than it should and smile. As I leave, the security guard is hauling himself up the last flight of stairs.

"Thanks."

I head down them and leave him cursing at the top. Drop my bike outside.

"One one, one one."

"One one, one one."

"One one, one one, POB X3, roger."

"You got 'em all on board, roger?"

"Roger."

"Okay, knock 'em out then, roger."

"Roger roge."

I'm tucking in the package into my bag, strapping my lock around my waist and generally preparing myself to ride off into the distance when the security guard comes bursting out of the door.

"What do you think you're playing at? I'll be calling your company and telling them what went on here. Who do you think you are? You can't just carry your bike into a person's office."

I let him finish his tirade as I look off into the eyes of an amazingly beautiful woman, long flowing hair and a complexion that makes me think that she must be from one of the Mediterranean countries, Italy, Spain, Greece, one of those. But for shame she can't see my eyes because of my Oakleys.

"Listen: this bike costs more than you take home in a week, so unless you're willing to pay for it when it gets stolen, don't be trying to act like you can tell me what to do."

With that stuck in his throat I'm off and out into traffic.

You get paranoid being a courier, there's nothing you can do to stop it or change it. Being a courier is like having some maddened, crazy old bastard slashing at you with a knife every day. After a few days you learn to be weary, you learn to protect yourself or you die. You get paranoid about everything, how much money you're getting paid, pedestrians, taxi drivers, whether it's going to rain, why Tottenham can never get a team together to win the league. Everything and anything. I'm paranoid because I have to be. I joke about it to people, but only other couriers know about that mixture of fear and adrenaline that courses through you when you've got to deliver a package and you've got the clock on you. When your controller's calling out the minutes to when you have to drop it off and it feels as if your whole life will be defined in that short space of time.

Everything is measured on the clock. How quickly you

pick up a package, how quickly you drop off a package. Time defines you because the more time that you save, the more money you make. Sometimes when I see couriers busting speed down Oxford Street I say to myself, They don't pay me enough to ride that fast. But I know that five minutes from now that will be me. Flying along the road at the limits of adhesion and screaming myself hoarse at pedestrians as they run like headless chickens into my path. Swearing at taxi drivers for doing U-ies without indicating, knowing that I could have been flying over that bonnet with my bike still attached to my feet. As a courier you learn that time is money.

No pain, no gain.

Everyone talks shop, you spend two-thirds of your life in a job, you work with people 24/7 who are doing the same job as you, what else do you talk about when you're not working? The independence of the former socialist republics that made up the Soviet Union and how it affects Europe? Like fuck. You talk about the day you had at work, the trivialities of it, everything that pissed you off and everything that made you smile. Then you go home and prepare for the next day. If you listen to conversations between couriers, invariably it will come round to how close you were to a crash today, or the really big crash you had last week. Danger is a prerequisite for this job, and we talk about it to keep that danger from consuming us. As if by telling our stories and reworking the myth of our brush with injury we will maybe make others and ourselves better able to cope with the next one.

I talk about crashes and smashes as much as any courier, but I've only told this story to a few. It's not for laughter and joking. Because all the stories we tell are a cathartic experience, through the telling we say, That wasn't so bad, and can go out there and do it again the next day.

Danny, my friend since school, he was with me and Iago when we used to bunk, he was the one that got me into riding. He always loved it. He was the first to get a BMX, the first to bunny hop, the first to race. He had his brother Joseph's Chopper as his second bike and I'd go round to his house and ride on it, feeling like nothing on earth could top this ever, not even sex. Which I'd heard and read so much about but had never tried. This. This was better than sex. We'd tear around the estate late at night, hollering and screaming, ducking down alleyways and wheelieing on the pavement. We'd pull apart his bike and put it back together, going around shops looking for parts to trick it out with. He was always the daredevil, taking risks that no one else would, jumping off walls, trying to bunny hop gates and stuff like that, and I'd try and follow, and through following I'd make myself do things. Stretch the edge of my experience and go for the rush.

Danny became a courier after me, he'd been busy at college, you know, A levels and all that. He came out on circuit with me during the summer, and he was dark. So fast and furious, never wondering what was going to come round the next corner, just going for it. We were the terrible twos, twelve and twenty-two. We'd ride like demons through traffic, racing each other. The one always trying to outdo the other. If I dropped off a package in ten minutes, he'd want to do it in nine. We'd spur each other on, and working for the same company it was just like we were back at school again. Like we were still on the estates, even though he'd moved because his parent's had divorced.

We'd gone into the West End to play some arcades, you know, go to Las Vegas or that place on Oxford Street, before the Trocadero became the place where callow youths with too much money and not enough sense became the arcade of choice in the centre of town. Busting speed along Oxford Street heading towards Tottenham Court Road, racing like demons, cutting in and out of the taxis, screaming our heads off and frightening the tourists, stepping into the road without looking. I took the inside when I should have got outside and Danny came past me like a train, looking back and giving me the finger. I jumped the curb, almost knocked down some shoppers and went tearing after him, screaming out his name and cursing under my breath as I got that gear turning. I saw the pedestrian step out and Danny drop his shoulder, slip around him and get clipped by a bus, which sent him into the side of a taxi.

When I got there he was still conscious and everything had stopped. The vultures had gathered to watch. A crowd was forming even, voices murmuring, and they all seemed to be entranced. As if Danny was someone famous and they were all in awe and the spell would only be broken once one of them touched him.

I held him until the ambulance came, it took forever. You know, seconds that just wouldn't move past, and they all stood there and watched me holding him. None of them moved or anything, just stood there. I told him everything was alright, that he'd be fine, and I was surprised by how little blood there was. I'd imagined that there would be lots and lots of blood, but there wasn't. Just some from his leg and arm where the skin had been torn off. They took him to hospital, I don't remember which one, maybe it was St Thomas's, that's the closest one, I think. I remember the ride in the ambulance, rocking and swaying and thinking that you could catch 'nuff speed if you were riding really close behind it, like you do when you draught buses, but you wouldn't have to stop for red lights. Sitting in the hospital, waiting for his parents to come, having people ask me questions about stuff I didn't know the answer to. Was he diabetic? Was he allergic to any drugs? Stuff like that, and I stared at them and couldn't understand why all these people weren't trying to help. What were they doing asking me questions when Danny was lying somewhere else all pale and limp? He'd slipped unconscious on the ride over and I'd thought that he'd died, but the ambulance man assured me he hadn't. But I remember that as the moment that he died, not three days later when his heart stopped for the third time and they called his time of death.

At his funeral, the priest said something banal and uninteresting about life and death, and all I could think about was the times we'd ridden down Oxford Street, cursing pedestrians, feeling that if I saw that pedestrian again I would kill him for what he did to my friend. That the fucker didn't have to step out when he did, he could have used a crossing like everyone else. But he had to be fast and try and duck out between taxis. Danny's mum gave me his old BMX, but I couldn't bear to see it every day, let alone ride it. So I gave it to his brother a few days later. I'd cry every time I had to walk past it. Now I'd like to have it back. He'd most probably give it back to me, but I've never had the courage to ask him for it.

In the first moment of peace I get in six hours of hard riding I head over to see Iago on Neal Street, the magazines rolled tightly into a pocket in my bag. Iago works in a clothes store, one of those trendy designer bastards with lots of space and light and a glass front open to the world and which has this huge swivel of a door that pivots open and takes up most of the front. How he found the job I do not know, but it must be one of the cushiest in the whole entire universe. All he does all day is DJ, which must be why he doesn't need to have a set in his house until now. The shop has him and another guy and some girl that also works as a sales assistant knock out the tunes for everyone to hear. And he gets paid two hundred a week for it. Not much else you can say really. The shop itself sells all the labels, Versace, Ralph Lauren, Moschino, etc., etc., *ad infinitum*. Everyone that works in there is so stuck up their own arses it's unbelievable. The amount of snotty-nosed bastards sticking their noses up in the air because you're not wearing designer gear gets on my tits.

Now if I had tits like that I wouldn't mind. My head swivels and I let out a growl. She looks, I shout.

"You know you love it really."

Then I'm past her and away, jumping the kerb and making the pigeons run from beneath my wheels. The only good thing you can say about his place of work is the amount of lovely, drop-dead, let-me-sniff-your-panties beautiful women that pass through its doors. It's like honey heaven, and that bastard Iago is there every day. The only thing that consoles me about this is the fact that they are all of the I'm-too-beautiful-for-my-own-good variety, which makes me smile every time I think about it.

Lock my bike up outside and walk in. Inside it's cool, if it didn't have air conditioning I would have been surprised. Iago's playing Faith, and feet are tapping as people sift through the clothes on display with assistants hovering in the distance, waiting to pounce. I'm given a few disapproving stares by some of the newbies, all stiff backs and *This is the first job where I get to dress nice all the time.* While those who know me nod or smile in my direction. I pull out the magazines and slap them on his record pile.

"One four, one four, where are you, Greer?"

The loudness of the radio startles everyone, makes them

jump and stare at me, their eyes locking onto me. Daring me to destroy their serene atmosphere once more. I turn it down and look expectantly at Iago as he tries to mix another song in. He holds up his hand in a wait gesture, so I twiddle my thumbs and look around, stepping over to some jackets. They're puffers by DKNY. Look at the price tag, three hundred and ten notes. Think about it for a moment. Slip off my bag and try it on. It looks ridiculous with my shorts and my legs bulging from the bottom of it, but I try to imagine myself wearing it with jeans on and think maybe the price could be overcome. I swing it back onto its hangar and zip it up. Mum told me to always leave things as you found it, so I do.

Iago's slipped it into Mary J's *My Life*.

"So what you saying?"

"Nothing."

"Okay, I'll go then."

"Yeah really."

"You're not going to let me ride here on my lunch break and then not talk to me."

"Yep."

"Bastard."

"You see that girl over there?"

"Where?"

"Standing by the jeans, light skin, with the Chinese eyes. She is fine."

"Ain't she a bit small for you? I know you like your tall women."

"Don't matter how tall she is when she's that fine."

I look at the girl again, smooth skin, a lovely olive colour, untouched by make-up. She's wearing Timberlands, things could be worse. But she's got long hair. One on the debit side. Girls with long hair should be avoided. Any girl that has hair long has nothing to do all day except flick it out of her face and annoy all the people that walk too close within her range. Stare at the cream top and those fake riding pants with the patch or the seam on the inside of the thighs and calves. In her hand she's carrying a carry case with a strap that has Leica woven into it. Iago's right, she is fine, really, really fine.

"Someone's calling you."

"What?"

"Your radio."

I hear it now. Peter's voice rolling my number into a litany as precise and bored as anyone who has ever had to repeat a name or a word can get.

"One one, one one, one one, one one, one one, one one."

He ends the last one on a long plaintive note that goes on forever, as I turn up the volume and speak into it.

"One one, one one."

"Where've you been?"

"Assaulting sheep."

"Don't get cocky with me. You've got two packages at Bishops, an EC1 and an E2, call me when you've got them onboard, roger."

"Roger roge. Fuck! I hate Bishops."

"What's wrong with them?"

"When you see the packages you have to carry, then you know what's wrong with them."

I pull out my sheet and quickly scribble the name down and the destination, putting down how much each drop will bring me. I like to keep a running total of how much I'm making. Makes totting it up at the end of the day a lot easier and quicker.

"I'll see you later, yeah?"

"Yeah."

I move to the door, pulling my Oakleys low across my eyes, flicking a glance across at the light-skin honey by the jeans. She's intent on looking for something her size, but as I look I can make out the darkened skin that surrounds her nipple through her top and feel myself stiffen as I walk.

"Eder!"

"What?"

Half-turn and wait for Iago to get it out.

"Party tonight, some record company thing, we're on the guest list."

"We're not playing?"

"Nah."

"Where?"

"Don't know the name of it, it's on Kingly Street. I'll come for you about ten, eleven."

"Best make it eleven."

"Okay, later."

I wave my hand in assent and leave, quickly unlocking my bike and saddling up. Staring at the girl as I ride off before my attention is captured by some fool pedestrian couple walking hand in hand at least a foot apart down the centre of the street.

"Wakey, wakey."

They scatter like the pigeons did, and I'm smiling as I slip into traffic.

I walk my bike back into Clerkenwell Green and sit down beside Greer and one-seven Martin.

"Good day?"

"Not too bad."

"How much you make?"

"Done about sixty."

"And you, Martin?"

"About seventy."

"So how much have you done?"

"About the same, and it's not even four o'clock yet. The day is still young."

Usually riders don't get into groups like this too often unless it's one of the major way stations like Soho or Covent Garden, but Peter likes to keep us together, it's been that way since I started. Whenever he can, and when work permits, he gets us together in one place, either here in the Green, Soho Square or sometimes Finsbury Circus further down in the city. I think it's as much to let himself know where we are as for our benefit. It creates a feeling of community amongst the riders. We like to go out sometimes after work on a Friday for a few drinks in the West End, which usually turn into all-night drinking sessions. I'm a new initiate into the pub routine, whereas all the other white boys on circuit have been doing it for years. I'm used to bringing a bottle and nursing a drink for a night. Buying drinks in clubs rather than in pubs where you can sit and have a chat and a laugh. In my personal opinion, more black people should do it, but you can't cut through years of cultural differences immediately, so I try to introduce those that I know to it and let it filter on from there.

"What's been happening to you lately, Martin? I haven't seen much of you on circuit."

"Went on holiday to Ibiza with me girlfriend."

"Good or bad?"

"It was great. I went out with my friends, she went out with hers, came back and shagged like bunnies."

"I can see you now, Martin, but I can't quite envision you as a bunny."

"What you been doing lately?"

"Same old, same old."

"Still riding three days?"

"Yeah, can't be riding five, too much hassle. As long as I make 250 a week I'm not bothered."

"Know what you mean, I've been thinking about only doing four days."

"Don't let Peter hear you say that."

"Yeah, I know, he'll give me his 'We need all the full-time riders we can get, I only let them ride those days 'cause they've been with the company for a long time' speech."

"But we have all of a year and a half, on you. We've got seniority."

"I hope when I'm with the company as long I can do three days."

"It's not just the time we've been with the company, it's how long we've been riding. We're veterans. You and one-five Terry are just new boys, whipper snappers."

"You forgot one-nine Paul and one-two Noel."

"Oh yes, I did, forgive me."

"Anyone want a smoke?"

Martin passes the box of Silk Cut around. I usually don't smoke on circuit, treating myself to a long spliff at the end of a hard day, or sometimes even a spliff and a bath at the same time. But that's for special occasions. But I take the cigarette that he's offering, free up with the freeness, and light it quickly with my clipper.

"What we doing Friday?"

"Have no idea."

"Aren't we doing anything?"

"Nah, a lot of the guys have stuff planned."

"Oh, looks like I'll have to amuse myself then."

"Thought you did that already."

Puff gently on the cigarette, feeling the nicotine rush, light up my forehead. Even though the sun's beating down on it, it feels as if there's a cold breeze circulating just around my cranium. Flick some ash away and watch the wind catch it and blow it back onto me.

"Saw this programme on reincarnation last night, fucking top programme."

"Yeah, I saw it too, about some woman who thought she was some Victorian chamber maid."

"Yeah, they took her back using... what's it called? Shit!"

"I think it's regression under hypnosis."

"Yeah, that's it. Fucking great it was, with her sitting in a trance telling this hypnotist all this stuff that she shouldn't have known."

"Spooky."

"Just like *The X-files* but in real life."

"Do you believe in *The X-files*?"

"Not the show, but yeah, I believe there are things out there people can't control or imagine. You know, the unexpected."

"Maybe."

"No, not maybe. I was round my friend's house and we were up listening to the radio, this was about when I was fifteen, maybe sixteen. Anyway, we're up listening to the radio when we hear this noise coming from downstairs. But we know there's no one in the house except us, the rest of his family went out that night. So we went downstairs and checked, thinking it was a burglar or something. But there was nothing there, turned on the light and everything. Looked everywhere. We were just about to go upstairs when this hum started and it just got louder and louder and then every window in the front room just blew in. They just exploded, almost blinded my friend, and there was never any explanation for it, ever."

We sit in silence and digest the story, puffing gently on the cigarettes, then Greer, ever the skeptic, jumps in.

"Could it have been a sonic boom, you know, low-flying aircraft and all that?"

"The insurance people thought about that, but he wasn't living near any aircraft bases or anything like that. They could never explain it. They said it must have been a freak accident. But my friend moved out soon after, couldn't stand to be in that house anymore."

"One one, one one."

"One one, one one."

"Three packages from Savage and Best EC4 going to Ecclestone SW8, roger."

"Roger roge."

"Shit, he's feeding you today, isn't he?"

"Don't worry, tomorrow he'll feed someone else, it's Peter's egalitarian nature."

"Egaliwhat?"

"It means someone who likes to spread the wealth around."

"Oh."

"I'll see you later."

"What time is it?"

"Half four."

"Later."

The bastard thing about being a courier, apart from taking your life in your hands every day, is the size of the packages they give you to carry. They seem to expect men on pushbikes to be able to carry packages that only vans could lug around town. You know, you get this huge fucking A0 portfolio that you've got to take into the West End, and all the time that you're riding you feel as if you're going to take off. Reach for the skies. You're afraid to go to hard round corners in case it slips sideways and takes you with it. You won't crash through that gap because you're afraid the package'll get caught on something and flip you sideways. Which is not good. Not good at all. So you're riding around more worried about the package than the traffic ahead of you and all the time you've got this fierce pain in your back from where it's grinding into your spine, you can't get rid of it because the pain is the most intense when you're in your natural riding position. You can't get off your bike to adjust it, because the clocks on you. You can't adjust it while you ride, because you'll lose control and take yourself to the kerb. So you grit your teeth and bear it and bitch like hell to the other couriers when you see them. What really burns is that no one ever offers a thank you. It's like, You're getting paid to deliver this package so you'll get no sympathy from me. To which you think, If that's the way you want it, whenever I have to bring you a package that says do not bend, the fucker will be as small as a postage stamp by the time you get it. Believe.

You always get heavy packages when someone wants to race you, and to keep up the pride of the outfit you have to kick speed and show them who's the boss, even though you want to scream out in agony and just rest on a grass verge somewhere. Sometimes the most enticing thing in the world is a soft patch of grass and a long spliff. You can't do that in the winter, you're too busy trying to keep your balls from freezing off and getting all the water out of your socks for that. Which is why I love the summer. The intensity of it all, the heat, the sun, the slowness of it. Slow like honey, heat that slows you down makes you lethargic, and all you want to do is fall asleep under its glowing rays. There have been a few times when I have just laid back in some square somewhere and gone to sleep and not heard jobs coming in. I don't do that now. Too much money would be lost, but back then it didn't seem so bad.

But summer is the best time to ride, because there is so much to see. The whole city is naked. Suddenly, as if by magic, all the beautiful women move forth and you wonder, Where were you in the winter when I needed a bit of a boost, where were you indeed? Because they come out and it's just a pleasure to watch them, throw the odd comment their way, see them smile, see them flirt. Because you know and they know that in the end it means nothing. You're riding, she's walking, nothing will come of it. But it's nice to know you are wanted, desired. Nothing makes a woman more attractive than for her to show a man that she wants him in the worst possible way. Inflation of the ego, but true nevertheless. I love it. When it's summer, couriering is the easiest job in the world. Easy as pie. If you like that sort of thing.

I'm sitting in the office, the fans on full blast. Peter's got three behind him, while Marilyn, Joan and Derek have a huge one wafting cool air over them. Take another sip of my water and watch the phones light up as customers ring in jobs. Marilyn, Joan and Derek write out the job on a slip of paper, fold it and then put it in a little chute that slides its way into Peter's glass booth. Microphone in front of him, a map of London under the Plexiglas on his table and another on the wall to his left. He's sweating, even with the fans on, circles of sweat staining his T-shirt. His bike, a Cannondale racer M700, leans beside me and I play idly with the tassel hanging from the handlebars. I only came in to hand in my sheets for last week.

If I don't, I don't get paid, and we can't be having that, not at all. A young man's got to have his money coming in on a regular basis, otherwise how is he to go out, pick up the chicks and more importantly, buy his records.

"One two, one two."

"One two, one two."

The reply is breathless, Noel must be riding fierce on his fixed-wheel, low-profile track bike. You get on that thing and it's so low to the ground it gets you scared. It is just a dark ride once you get that gear going. He's got a fifty-two thirteen if I remember rightly.

"Head over to Marshall's EC2, they've got two packages going to W4, roger."

"Roger roge."

"Call me once you're POB, got more details for you."

"Roger roge."

Peter leans back in his chair, sticking out the slight pot belly he has gained over the last few months. His dark skin gleaming underneath the layer of sweat. He runs a hand across his bald scalp, then flicks his nose a few times with his first two fingers. Making a semi drum roll. A habit which annoys everyone. Before settling back in and leaning in towards his microphone.

"One seven, one seven, where are you, Martin?"

"One seven, heading down Fleet Street towards Blackfriars, roger."

"Roger roge, keep coming toward the city, roger."

"Roger roge."

Look at my watch: quarter to six. Not long before knocking-off time, wonder whether I should go now or just sit in the office and wait for another job. Look at my sheet for today lying in my lap and tot up the numbers along the side. Made just over eighty today on twenty-seven drops, which is good.

With the bonus, if I keep doing the same amount of work, I should bring in about 290 for this week. Not bad at all. For a small company, Peter pays well, and if we're making this much money, Peter must be pulling in a load more. Pick up my bag and stick my head around the screen.

"Peter, I'm going now, yeah?"

"What do you mean going? You've got fifteen minutes left."

"What's fifteen minutes, man?"

"Do you know how many jobs could come in in those fifteen minutes. You sit your arse down and wait till six."

"Okay, okay."

Pick up a paper and flick through it. One of the broadsheets. I can't stand tabloids, maybe some of my mum has rubbed off on me. Turn it to the music section, look through their reviews, see if there's anyone I know of that's being reviewed just so I can take the piss out of some whiter boy commenting about a music he has no knowledge of. Middle-class white boy gone to university to become a journalist and now he's writing about Snoop or Dye or the Wu Tang. Turn the page and see a review of that club Speed. Saying how jungle is now intelligent and progressive. Stop myself from dismissing it and read some more. Doesn't say much about the atmosphere, just that you should check it out to find out more about jungle, if you're into that sort of thing. Feel to chuck the paper in the bin, but instead turn it back around and place it nicely back where I found it. Me and Iago did pass by that club a few weeks back, whole load of victims out to listen to jungle, not one black face amongst them. If that's jungle, I ain't up for it. All speed is is a club where white people can listen to jungle without fear of being in a club full of niggas. All you can do is shake your head and wonder what the fuck is going on when music gets segregated like that. When those who are into the music but not the crowd can split it in two like that. What's wrong with us, you feel like saying. What, ain't we white enough?

Then we go ahead and take over Samantha's on a Thursday night, when all the young junglists come out. With the flashy clothes and the expensive labels, and the atmosphere is just pure blackness. Just pure uninhibited enjoyment. Grin at the thought of those nubile young bodies dancing under the strobing lights.

Look again at my watch and see only a few minutes have crawled by. Peter's calling out instructions to Greer and I feel like a spliff, but Peter frowns on that sort of thing.

"Marilyn, can I ponce a fag?"

"Yeah."

"Thanks."

Marilyn smokes Marlboro Lights, which isn't too bad, I'm just glad she don't smoke B&H or Regal. Take one and offer her another, but she shakes her head. She's busy typing up a spreadsheet on one of the four Macs that are in the office. Light it and puff away contentedly as time idles by. Watch Peter, his big face staring intently down at the map as he chews on some chewing gum, fingers tapping some rhythm only he can fathom on the desk. Turn and look out the window at the buildings opposite, try to look inside, see if I can see anyone else. But I quickly get bored and start shifting on my seat like a naughty schoolboy.

I hate waiting to leave work/It's better when you're out on circuit, you know, you can sit with the lads have a chat. But when you're in the office there is no escape. You just have to wait it out, wait it out. Keep staring at the clock, hoping it will move just a little bit faster, just a bit, come on, just do it once for your uncle Eder. Stub out the cigarette and twiddle my thumbs, purse my lips and mentally try to force time to move faster.

"Got one for you to take you home."

"What is it?"

"Hollings on Old Street going to Utica NW1."

"Since when do I live in Camden?"

"Do you want it or not?"

Write down the details and glare at the back of Peter's head. Always giving me these fucked jobs when it's time to be going home. Pull on my bag and duck out down the stairs.

I cut inside a taxi and belt it down towards Euston. I want to hit Gower Street running and do the demon run, down Charing Cross Road and around Trafalgar Square. That is a run and a half, 'cause if you catch the lights right you can boot it all the way down to Westminster without stopping. It is the living rush. Draught a bus for a few seconds before its brake lights flash. Slip outside it and dive through a gap between the bus and a lorry along its side. Head for the left and keep the pace high. The only thing about the bike that is mildly annoying is the thumbshifters, though they never give me problems. I'd rather have Rapidfire plus, the underbar shifters that Shimano brought out a few years back which you move with your thumb and forefinger. For me anyway, it feels like you've got greater control of the bike and what it's doing. I've been meaning to buy a pair for a while, because Shimano replaced all their rapid-fire changers over to gripshift, which is a pig to use after a while.

Come up to a set of lights, brake and bounce the back wheel. Not to be done in the wet, but in the dry it stops you in half the distance, and I've always been prone to sliding the back wheel, which doesn't do your tyre any favours. Though it does scare the shit out of pedestrians when you haul up to a set of lights and skid in sideways.

Take my foot out of the pedal and sit on my top tube while I wait for the lights to change and watch a courier across the way from Metro perch like a nigga. Front wheel cocked to one side, feet seesawing the pedals to keep him steady. I used to do that, but after I got into the spds I started to eat gravel. Coming up to lights and trying to perch, then when I felt that I couldn't hold it no more, sticking my foot out. Or trying to, because I couldn't get my foot out and I'd lean gently over to one side and collapse in a heap on the floor. My ego destroyed as the cars behind me beeped their horns because the lights had just changed.

I watch him them dismiss him, he ain't saying nothing on his fixed wheel. Lights change and I turn the big gear as he slips out in front. I'm not worried because I'll catch him within a few hundred yards. Riding isn't just about acceleration, it's about sustained speed. Keeping the rhythm flowing, turning that gear all the time at the same pace. Riding is about gaining momentum and keeping it. Which, if I do say so myself, I do rather well. Pull in a few yards behind him and keep up with him as we head for the lights. See them start to change and he's not slowing. Look for a gap to my right, duck in between two cars and jump the lights s just as they turn red. Swinging the bike as I shove my arse further back onto the saddle. Take a hard cut inside some slowing traffic, squeeze my brakes slightly and ease inside. Don't bother with looking behind me. I'm not worried with what he's doing. He's either with me or he's not. Just concentrate on my riding.

Jump across New Oxford Street and swing her down onto Shaftesbury Avenue. Carry on up, passing car after car as they sit waiting. Go up a slight incline but don't change gear, push it hard. Feel my breathing come smooth and loose. Lights are starting to change and the cars at Cambridge Circus are turning right still. Not enough space to take the corner on the inside. So I cut out to the right and slash in front of the lead car, bike keeled so far over I can feel the reflected heat from the pavement. Horns go behind me as I stick my foot out and use it as a brake, because if I pull anything I'm going to flip.

Then I'm barrelling down Charing Cross Road, head to the inside, and feel the need to change. Move my thumb across, hearing and feeling the click as I change gear, let my feet hold still for a moment then kick it in and feel that added resistance as the gear takes hold. Zoom across the lights by the Hippodrome, screaming, "Wakey wakey, hands off Snakey."

Shift my hands slightly and lower my head. When I was younger I used to do all of this anaerobically. I would ride really fast but without taking oxygen in, just using that which was stored in my body, and no matter how fast I breathed as I rode I would just tire because I'd go into oxygen debt. Doesn't happen anymore. Kick the gear round even faster and duck inside some tourists trying to make up their minds about how to use the zebra crossing. Almost to Trafalgar. Zoom into it and keel to the right, keeping my eyes on the taxis outside of me that want to turn in. This is where I did my collarbone the second time around when I went over the bonnet of one of those fuckers. He said he couldn't see me, which was bollocks. That destroyed the Marin Bear Valley that I'd only brought a few weeks earlier. Buckled the front wheel, nearly bent the frame in half. I didn't ride for a good couple of months.

Straighten out, cut in between two cars. Frighten some more pedestrians at the zebra crossing and go gutting it down and away past Nelson's Column. Swing right, then left and I'm away and heading towards Westminster. A bus pulls out and I'm in there behind it, head down, knees pumping. Shift another gear to keep up. Buses make such a big hole in the air that you can draught behind 'em forever. Take a quick look up to check the brake lights and see there's a group of people staring out the back at me and pointing. Flick my eyes down to the brake lights again, then back to them. Don't take any notice of them, blank them from my mind.

The lights flash and I'm hard up against the back end of the bus, have to really work to pull out and around as it pulls to the inside. Feel that wall of air shove me in the chest as I depart the secure warmth of the back of the bus. Out of the corner of my eye I can see those people who were watching me out of the back of the bus moving to a window along the side to watch me sprint past.

Coming up to Westminster I sit up straighter in the saddle, change a few gears and brake slightly. The traffic's heavy here and most of it's stationary. Pick a channel and rush down it, pumping the brakes as I go. Get down to the lights and they're all there. The commuters, all sitting spread out across the lights. Some with their trousers fastened with bicycle clips at the bottom. Some wearing shorts, some with panniers, with dayglo red bags hanging off the front wheel. Some on racers, most on mountain bikes. Slide up behind a big gaggle of them over on the inside and wait for them to jump as soon as the lights change.

An old biddie on her fixed wheel with a woven basket at the front of her frame comes through the massed ranks of cars and decides to jump the lights. Slowing down and edging her bike forward until she thinks the traffic's clear, then getting up out of her seat and turning that gear as hard as she can. It's commuters like her that give couriers a bad name. But the police don't haul her over. No, just anyone with a bag and a radio. I've been pulled over four times in the last month alone, and fined twice: for jumping a red light and riding the wrong way down a one-way street on the pavement. The fucking thing was, I wasn't even riding hard, just moving slowly ,looking for an address.

Watch her try to escape into the distance and know I'll have overhauled her before she even gets to the bottom of the hill, just as long as none of these clowns get in my way. In the mornings I usually don't mind if a commuter goes past, but in the evening it's a matter of pride. No one overtakes me. No one.

The lights change and they head off towards the horizon. Their legs churning round because they've started off in a really low gear. I let them go and just turn my gear. Pegging back each one in turn with ease. Just riding to the side of them, I cruise past, not even trying very hard. As they move their whole bodies in a show of exertion to get that little extra speed out of their preferred mode of transportation. I find them beneath my contempt and beyond redemption. So I leave them to their little tag and draught party and jump over the roundabout and down towards Vauxhall Bridge.

Sprinkler

We're walking along in the cool night air, the Moschino shorts I'm wearing flapping against my legs. Look down at the Darwin's on my feet and wonder why my foot twists slightly to the left every time I take a step. Iago's swinging round lamp posts as if he's Gene Kelly in *Singin' in the Rain*. Shove my hands into my pockets and scratch my bollocks for a second before pulling them out and taking a furtive sniff. The slightly musky scent of my bollocks reminds me of sweaty nights of passion. Maybe I should take out Louise, it might be fun, a little food, a little dance, some sex. Maybe. But I'm not sure what music she's into, and you know you have to know these things before you fuck. I've been out with a few girls before whose music I didn't like and you'd get into this power struggle thing where you'd play the music you liked whilst fucking at yours and the music they liked whilst fucking at theirs. Then you'd have to decide where to go out together, which type of music to listen to and one of you'd always be disappointed. Not that I'm into that mutual clubbing thing, just a bit too anal for me. If you're individuals with your own lives, why do you have to go out and do everything together. It is beyond me. Couples at clubs sucking face and generally annoying everyone around them by their lovey-dovey passion. Makes me want to puke.

I shiver at the thought of overly amorous couples snogging in clubs and move my thoughts away from the subject. You know there's only so many bad thoughts a head can contain. Run over to Iago and drag him from the lamp post, taking him to the ground. We struggle for a while. Shove my hand onto his throat and try to choke him while his hand sneaks ever closer to my bollocks. Lunge away from him laughing. Then straighten abruptly as I see a policeman watching us closely from his car. Look to Iago, who's brushing himself off and trying not to laugh. Grab a hold of his arm and pull him down the street to the club.

The club's halfway along Kingly Street, all black and gold wiring. The name's above the door but I don't bother with it. A club's a club, right? Not many people outside except for the few people that you always see gathered outside, those few who don't have tickets and those waiting for their friends to arrive. Staring eagerly at every face to see whether or not it is their friend. I stand behind Iago as he chats to the bouncer on the door, who ushers us to one side to see about us being on the guest list. A small white man, very thin, in a shirt with flared collars pulled over his leather jackets lapels, and the cuffs covering his hands, holds the guest list close to his chest.

"Yes?"

"We're on the guest list. Iago plus one."

The man looks at Iago strangely, as if to say, That's not your real name.

"Can you spell that for me?"

"Yeah, I-A-G-O."

White boy looks down the list, his pen now hanging from his lip as he chews on the end. Eyes locked to his sheet of paper. I shuffle my feet and wonder why it always takes so long for you to get in if you're on the guest list. Why they keep you waiting on tenterhooks for precious minutes when you could be inside drinking and dancing. Through the open door I can hear the opening riff of an old funk tune that I used to play before I went to sleep. Mum used to come in sometimes and dance to it before telling me to turn it off and go to bed. That wah, wah guitar has the blood flowing in me and I move a little, sway and shuffle my feet in time with the music. Iago has his hands thrust into the pockets of his jeans and his jaw is starting to jut out, as it does when he gets annoyed. The guest-list protector turns over the top sheet and starts to scan the next layer. Nods his head and pulls the pen out of his mouth.

"There you are."

Crosses out the names and hands us two small metal squares. As we walk in, the bouncer inside the door takes the squares from us and places them in a little tin beside him. What was the point. There's no search and we're ushered straight up some red stairs into the club. Turn a corner and before us stretches this huge cavern of a club as if it was under some railway arches. Down by the end wall, the floor dives downwards and I can vaguely see into the dance floor area. Out on the fringes the lighting is subdued, but as you get closer to the dance floor it becomes darker, more intimate. On the left is some kind of patio section with this fake ivy growing round it. Inside is a seating area where lots of people are sitting and talking, drinks gently turned and cigarettes held high in the air. The bouncer guarding the entrance has his arms crossed over his huge barrel chest and only opens them when a gold disc is flashed in his face similar to the ones that we handed to the guy on the outside.

The interior is quite full and I'm busy staring at the people closest to me, trying to figure out what they do and how well they do it. This far out no one's dancing, everyone's deep in conversation. The music is loud, but not as loud as I would have thought hearing it from the outside. It's at a nice level for conversation as well as dancing. I concede to myself that it's probably that way because we're so far away from the dance floor.

Iago grabs my arm and pulls me over to the floor and I lean on it in anticipation of being served. Even though we're by the end and we'll be last. After a few minutes of just standing, Iago takes matters into his own hands. Stands on the rail running round the bar at shin height, shoves his fingers into his mouth and whistles loud. The bar staff stop for a fraction of a second and everyone stares.

"I'll have a Budweiser and my friend will have…"

He looks to me and I hurriedly tell him what I want.

"Yeah, he'll have a double Archers on ice."

He steps back down and smiles contentedly.

"That got their attention. Ain't leaving me here down by the end and not serving me."

Gaze idly out at the crowd as I wait for the drinks to arrive and watch the Soho brigade strut their stuff. Their manner of dress annoys me. Look, I was born in the Seventies. I don't want to go back; apart from the fact that was the last time that Brazil won the world cup, and I was born, the Seventies don't hold that many good memories for me. Into that pool of good things, I have to retrospectively add funk, rare groove, the birth of hip hop and George Clinton. Apart from these things, the Seventies was a bad decade. You know, flares, disco, bad hairstyles, the Vietnam War, the destruction of the Black Panther Party, flares, Adidas Gazelles, those bastard Adidas shoe bags, blackxploitation and the myth and coolness of the pimp hustler that so many white folk want to buy into. The Seventies was just so full of bad things that it is just sinful to bring it back. But fashion is a bastard regurgitator of anything that has vaguely any history whatsoever. So interested in looking back at the past it doesn't know how to deal with the future, how to design for the future. Why do that when you can just reconstruct what has gone before.

Iago hands me my drink and I let it swirl around for a while. Let the ice cut into the harsh solidity of the peach schnapps. I've tried archers straight before and it burned the fuck out of my throat and slipped me into alcoholic oblivion faster than I would have liked. Iago offers his arm and I lead us into the throng of people, moving through the sifting sands of people who are standing or leaning as their bodies sway gently or move more rapidly with the music. Take up a position just off the dance floor, by an outcropping of the bar. I grab it with my elbow and lean on it, placing my drink beside me. Iago's out in front of me and moving in time with the funk.

Giving up food for funk,
giving up food for funk...

Sip from my drink and savour it as it goes down. Looking at the girls, I get the feeling that this will be a fun night. One of those nights out in a club where the girls are nice and if you wanted you could speak to them, get her digits and maybe something would come of it, but instead you drink a little and dance a lot. Enjoying the atmosphere and the bassline, without having that pressure to perform for a girl. To go over and ask, What's your name? What's your sign? One of those parties that for once you feel that maybe a girl's going to come up and say, "I find you very attractive."

And go from there.

Lift my head up from contemplating the ice swimming in my glass and how the clear liquid is becoming slightly cloudy. To contemplating the women. And for my viewing pleasure there are many of them. Some dancing, some not. Short skirts are all the rage, the thighs and calves, firm and taut. Their legs made firmer by the heels on their feet. Long sinewy arms move cigarettes in intricate circles in the air as they speak or dance. Feet moving back and forth, hips swaying, sinuously. For a second they become ghostly apparitions, formed from smoke and rolling across the room, their human bodies sinking to the floor like a second skin. Blink and refocus and see them as they appear in my normal waking life. The beautiful people. The ones that are talked about in the style rags, the arbitrators of fashion and fashionability. Or are they just followers? Black people are dotted amongst the white glitterati. I see them, and every time I meet an eye I nod my head in acknowledgement and keep on looking. Iago has drifted off into the crowd, maybe looking for a girl, I don't know. He's sly like that. I think he feels that he can't be too obvious otherwise I'll deny him the chance to make it with whoever he's lusting after.

Twist my neck from side to side to get rid of the stiffness which seems to be accumulating there. Wish I could get a massage to ease it properly. Turn and look into the mirror that is behind the bar. Look at myself and try to see what girls see in me. I know I'm not unattractive, but just standing here looking in the mirror I can see a whole load of guys that if I was a woman would make me wet. But looking at them again, a lot of them seem too wrapped up in the artifice of masculinity. The musculature, the body and how it is shown or adorned. Too many man with his chest out of doors and his stomach hard and defined from hours in the gym. Muscles bulging beneath tight white cotton T-shirts and tight jeans designed to delineate your bell end. After a while you wonder what's the point of it all. I'm never going to look like that, so why bother if that's what women want? Because that's who they chose to go out with. Rather than us nice caring black men that'll treat 'em right. But looks go before personality, live with it.

Look to my left and then to my right, nothing doing. Finish my drink and slap it down with a flourish, and turn to step down into the dance floor.

"'Scuse me, 'scuse me, 'scuse me, thanks."

Get down there and find I was right, the music is louder here than it is at the back. The DJ's slipped into something more modern. Nod my head and wave my hand in the air, palm flat and straight.

U will know,
oh, oh, u will know...

Sing with Black Men United and shift from one foot to the other. If I stand still for too long my back tightens up and gives me grief for the rest of the night. the only cure I've found for it is to dance most of the night and then sit for the rest of it. The curse of the dance floor soon strikes as I find myself being nudged here and there by people who take up too much space, and over in the corner I can see the almost inevitable contemporary dancer doing his own thing out of time with any song being played. Whilst his adoring public just stand in awe of his amazing physical prowess. See Iago caught in the embrace of a rather large woman, at least five foot ten, with a huge head wrap on that takes her to over six foot. He catches my eye and winks. I smile and nod back, wondering how she's going to fit her head wrap into the Mini.

The DJ slips it into the remix of "I Wanna Be Down", and I nod my head in sympathy to the beat. The DJ's good, nice mixes, not showy, "professional" is the word that springs to mind. A professional DJ. He's working the crowd, dropping the odd new tune in to keep everyone alert as well as playing the songs they've been listening to for the past few months, and you know he has to play the anthems. If he doesn't, he will be shot, and I know for a fact that at least a dozen people would have already gone up to him and requested he play them. People want to hear what they know, or what radio stations think they should know. That's why I love pirates: if we like it, we'll play it, and that's it, end of argument. No playlists, just one person's taste, one person's choice coming to you live and interactive. DJs have this habit of being forgetful, only playing what is around right at that second rather than anything that's more than six months old. It's part of that super heavy rotation around the club scene where a song gets played to death by the DJs then shoved into the box marked "Do not open until the turn of the century". I like a bit of variety, a bit of daring, the desire to go beyond what is the norm and expand some boundaries. But DJs are scared, want to keep the crowd happy, want to keep their jobs safe, and are unwilling to take risks. Me, I'm young and I don't care. I'll take as many risks as possible. Why not? It's not like I've got a reputation to protect or anything. I'm still too small time for that.

Method Man's got me open, and the vocals soaring over the top turn the dance floor into a hotbed of activity. Get turned around and see her standing at the top of the steps. The light-skin honey from the shop. She's in a big white blouse, which is tied in a knot around her stomach, showing her belly button. I peer into the darkness to see whether it's an innie or an outie, but can't make it out. From the waist down she's got a long jean skirt which buttons up the front, and apart from the top three, they're all undone. Revealing and concealing her legs, which I can just make out to be firm and taut. Her hair is tied up and wisps of it are framing her face. Whistle low under my breath and watch her standing there, arms crossed in front of her, one hand cupping the other elbow and her drink held in the other hand. Stand for a second wondering what to do. Do I leave it for a while, just watch her, or try and make the move now. You never know, the night is young, some other lovely might come my way and I'll be locked in conversation with her and unable to get away. Then the doubts come. What if she's like completely out of it? Just a pretty face?

I can't stand going out with unintelligent women, which is why I try not to go out to often with girls below nineteen. Because for one they don't really know what they want yet, but what they feel they want is a relationship, which I ain't down for. You're honest and you tell them this in the beginning and they say okay, then later down the line they slap you with it. How you deceived them and lead them on. Second, they ain't done nothing with their life yet, they haven't travelled, they haven't expanded their outlook, broadened their minds.

It's one of the things that I am most grateful to Mum for. The fact that she took me and Juli with her on holiday and we didn't just go to places and stay in the hotel by the pool and do all the activities the brochure recommended. We went out and ate in local restaurants, struggled with the language, drove up into the hills. That's why Juli's off roaming Europe right now, 'cause Mum instilled that traveller's instinct in her. I might just be a courier, but I've travelled and seen places beyond London, whereas little miss South London ain't done nothing yet. She thinks travelling to Luton or Birmingham is an experience.

And thirdly they ain't got no money, and if they do, it ain't much. I don't mind paying, but when you have to pay all the time and they expect you to, then I have to say hold it. I ain't shelling out no more cash on you if you're not willing to reciprocate. You have to lay down the law and let it be known where you stand, otherwise you get fucked, big time.

I think about leaving it, but I keep twisting to look at her as she stands there up on the stairs. I know I'm being obvious but there's nothing I can do about it. So I decide, Get it over with. As I walk toward her I'm thinking, What do I say? Don't say nothing stupid or forgettable. I gots to be in there in the first line otherwise, unless she's receptable, I'm gonna get kicked to the kerb. Climb the steps in front of her and look her dead in the eye, open my mouth to say something when the DJ wheels the song back, the daemon sound echoing round the club and an intro slides in. All eerie violins and bassline. I'm stopped in my tracks, my mind's spinning, memories of hearing this song a long time ago. Hearing it and loving it. It was one of those songs that I thought I would remember forever. You know the one that you always remember the words to because you've played it so many times and sung it forever. I never had a copy of it on vinyl. I taped it off the radio, and you know cheap TDKs: it fucked and I hadn't copied it to another tape. It was gone, but I carried it with me. Already I'm anticipating the chord change and the moment the drums kick, all energy and life. The drummer snapping his wrists and getting them smoking.

My eyes must have glazed over, because they refocus and I'm looking into some girl's face. A mixture of oriental and black features, olive skin and long black hair, with slanted eyes curving upward, full high cheekbones, a rather broad nose with flared nostrils and full lips. But for the life of me I don't know what I'm doing in front of her.

She tilts her head to one side and looks quizzically at me. I shrug, shake my head.

"Sorry."

I mumble and move back down the steps to get to the DJ booth. It's like I'm in a dream and nothing is real or substantial.

I see the booth, and start to move towards it, sliding through the crowd, singing the song as it plays. So fast paced and the woman's voice is haunting, so full of pain and passion. Emotion layered over emotion as if she has seen so much and all of it has been distilled into the purity of sound coming from her throat. I'm moving faster through the crowd, knowing I have to know what this song is called. I have to know. My life depends on it.

An alarm goes off, then the music cuts out and we lose all the lights. People don't know what the fuck is going on. Water pours down from the ceiling. Everyone's screaming and shouting and running towards the exits. But to me this is just a heavy fog around me, nothing exists except that record and getting to the booth. Push back against the tide that is moving against me. Force my way to the booth, where the DJ's busy shoving his records into his carry cases.

"What was that record you just played?"

"What?"

"What was that record you just played?"

"Are you insane or something, the place is on fire."

"What was it called?"

I don't know it but I'm shouting at him and gesturing. He grabs his cases and shoves past me. I grab his arm, and the box he's carrying knocks the breath out of me. I go down to one knee, but I'm still holding onto his jacket.

"What was the record called?"

"Get off me!"

He kicks out at me and his foot slides across my chest. He almost falls but recovers his balance just in time as I let go and try to regain my breathing. He picks up the box that slipped out of his hands and sprints towards the exits. While I sit there, feeling the pain in my side throb and sharp spikes of agony spear my flesh. The water sputters and comes to a halt. The dripping of water onto the floor is hard in my ear as I shiver wetly. Faintly, off in the distance, I can hear the wail of sirens.

Obsession

I wake up, strange sounds surround me, already I'm burning under the sheets. Throw my arm out and brush them from my body. Let my body cool, even though I know within a few minutes I'm going to be hot again. Light's pouring through my window, scouring my eyes even through my closed lids. Twist my head to one side, open my eyes a crack and sneak a peek at my watch. Twelve. Not good. Shake my head and feel the rawness in my throat, and the sniffles in the back of my nose. Summer colds are the worst. Think back on last night and cringe, shudder and feel the embarrassment wash over me again. I must have been mad. Trying to find out the name of that song when everyone around me was trying to get out of someplace about to be consumed by fire. I didn't even get out till Iago came and dragged me out. Having had enough sense to leave in the first place.

Turn onto my front and bury my head in the pillow. Idiot. The word swirls in my head as I spell it out, spell it backwards. Toidi. My mind keeps saying it over and over and over, like a scratched record. Shake my head despairingly at the weak joke I've just made. Not good at all. Wonder what I should do now. This is my day off. Who to see, what to do? Twist round again on the bed, finding it extremely uncomfortable and not in the least bit conducive to lightening my mood of self-pity and loathing.

How could I have been so stupid. Then I think about the girl. Me standing in front of her with my mouth open and my eyes glazed over. I want to die. Just take me now God, just take me now. The only thought that gives me any comfort is the fact that I'll never see her again and my shame will never be revealed.

Cross my arm over my face and breathe out. Expelling all the air from my lungs. I need to talk to someone, get this shit off my chest. One of the few things that I learned from counselling after Danny died. Pull my phone off the little table near my head and put it on my chest. Dial the number and listen to the rings.

She picks it up after the seventh one, sounding breathless.

"Hello."

"Hi, it's me."

"Oh hi, how you doing?"

"Not good, not good at all."

"Why?"

"Just had one of the worst experiences of my life, that's all."

In the background I can hear the baby struggling to be free, making baby noises and parts of words.

"Listen, I'm looking after the baby at the minute, the bitch has gone out again, come round and tell me about it."

"Okay, what time you want me round?"

"How urgently do you need to talk?"

"I'll be round in the next half hour."

"Okay, see you later."

"Later."

Put down the phone and feel better already. Khadija always could do that to me. Lie in bed for a few more seconds before getting out and heading for the bathroom. Pull off my boxers and chuck 'em into the laundry basket by my door, pad down the corridor naked and step into the shower. Turning it on full blast. The burning hot water searing my skin as I try to eradicate all thoughts of last night through the purification of hot water. Hoping that this penance will cleanse me of my shame. The water cuts through me, making me want to scream, but I stay under the jet, my fingers turning white as I hold onto the taps. Bow my head and let the pain come. The water rages around me, the cubicle fills with steam. I stand there, head lowered, biting my bottom lip until I can't take anymore, not a second more. Turn the taps quickly and reduce the heat level to one that is more tolerable.

Open the new packet of Lemsip and shake it into the cup before smothering it under a good half inch of honey and pouring in the hot water. Stand there wrapped in my towel and sip quickly from the mug. I can't be getting a cold, it takes too much energy from me. Whenever I get one I revert to my pre-teen days when my only relief from colds was to lie in bed and let Mum mother me. If a cold progresses too far, I still want that to happen, so I try and nip them in the bud so that I don't crumble into some weak, snivelling child again.

Finish the drink and start counting out the various vitamins that I'll be taking for the next few weeks. Usually I just take a few, but I think this calls for something a bit extra. Multivitamins, iron supplements, cod liver oil. Grab the juice by the empty mug, slip the tablets into my mouth and wash them down with it.

Walk back into my room and pull on my cycling gear. I don't feel like playing anything, but I do anyway. Something mournful by Roberta Flack. Her voice reminds me of the one in the song, which flashes me back to that soaking-wet club and my voice shouting out.

"What's this record called? I really need to know."

Pull my bike out from the wall and slip on my Oakleys and out of my front door, leaving the record playing behind me.

Khadija's been my friend for a long time now. I find that she gives me the female perspective. I don't have many female friends. Maybe women sense something about me that I haven't discovered yet. Something dangerous and sinister. I've known Khadija for about six years, she was the best friend of my first real girlfriend. You know, intensity of emotion, puppy love. That burned me up for a while. And whilst I've lost contact with her, I've kept in contact with Khadija. Glad I have too, she's steered me through some rough times. Her parents are Asian, though they came to England by way of Kenya, she's got a younger sister who got herself pregnant and leaves Khadija and her mother to look after it for her. You know sixteen-year-olds. Think they own the world.

Khadija lives on the other side, over by Clapham, so I decide to do a quick run around the common to ease out some of the tension that is wound up inside me. It feels good to race the wind. The sun beating down as I slip past cars and take the turns hard, my thighs burning with the exertion. I'm trying not to breathe hard, but I do as I try to ride the frustration out. Cut in front of a Beamer at a set of lights, who leans on the horn, I give him the finger and ride on, turning that big gear round. My upper body as still as I can get it, the only movement my pistoning legs. Beside me a horn goes off. Look to the side, it's the BMW up beside me, the passenger window down and the driver, a middle-aged businessman, leaning over and shouting at me.

"What the fuck do you think you're doing? Do that again and I'll run you over."

I look at him, wondering what he's under. He must be one of those road-rage people. Ignore him and carry on riding. But what he said sticks in my head. Come up beside him at the lights ahead and tap on his window. He looks surprised to see me, most probably wondering how I caught up with him so quickly. Motion for him to wind down his window. Pull a big one and spit directly into his face.

"It's fuckers like you that give idiots a bad name."

He's in shock as I cut right and down onto Khadija's street. Look back over my shoulder and see him trying to change lanes to follow. But the traffic's too thick. Chief. Pull up in front of Khadija's house and ring the bell. She finally arrives with baby on her shoulder and I hug her long and hard. Khadija's just over five feet tall, so I have to bend a ways to get to her. Her long hair is tied in a ponytail and her face as usual has that excited look that small kids get when they're just about to open presents. She is the most excitable person I've ever met, and she is also the most beautiful. She has a soul that would make an angel weep with joy. Totally giving. Which is why she gets such a hard time from her sister, who's always taking liberties. Don't get me wrong, when push comes to shove, she'll kick you to the kerb. But in such a nice way that you thank her for it.

"How you doing?"

"Better. Just got the small one off to sleep. Come in."

She turns and I pull my bike inside placing it so it doesn't scuff the walls. Take off my gloves and pad into her kitchen to tear myself off some kitchen roll so I can wipe the sweat off my face. She comes in a few moments after without baby and sits herself at the kitchen table.

"Okay, so what's wrong?"

I stand and tell her my whole sad story; she just nods and doesn't utter a word until I pause for breath and ask, "Do you have anything to drink?

"Yeah, there's some orange juice in the fridge."

"What do you think?"

"I think it fits the profile."

"What profile?"

"The profile that is you. Everyone's got a profile. If you were looking at mine, you'd see twenty-two-year-old self-confessed bong queen who loves to smoke. Intelligent overachiever. Oldest girl, so therefore taken to mothering. Sexually frustrated by her lack of attractiveness to members of the opposite sex."

"Come on, you've had plenty of boyfriends."

"Yeah but they've all been bastards and just out for a quick fuck. But let me finish. Under no pretences about the world, but also wholly optimistic. A bad combination at the best of times. In short, a twentieth-century female."

"And me?"

"You? Well you're a risk-taker, even moreso since Danny died. You feel you have to take his place, keep up his standards. You always looked up to Danny. You're insecure, intelligent though you try very hard to conceal it behind your 'Never went to college, never went to uni' exterior. Easily hurt, very sensitive and all-round good guy. If guys can be good, that is."

Take a sip of the orange juice and nod my head in her direction for an accurate assessment of my personality.

"How do you fit what happened last night into my profile?"

"You're an obsessive. Most men are. You know, toys for the boys and all that. More inclined to get emotional about inanimate objects rather than living, breathing people. How would you feel if someone totalled your bike? You'd want to kill them, right? Or if someone stole your record collection."

"Yeah, but…"

"No buts. This is a sweeping generalisation, but usually true: men form relationships with objects, women with other women and other people."

"Okay, so say for argument's sake I believe you, what do I do now?"

"You find the record. You've got to after what you put yourself through last night."

Take another sip.

"That was what you were going to do anyway, right?"

"Yeah."

"Well, end of argument then."

"So what you been doing then?"

"Looking after baby, looking for a job. You know, the usual."

"What's the point of going to university if you can't get a job?"

"Expand your outlook on people. You meet lots of different people at uni, makes you more able to deal with life, exposes you to lots of different outlooks and perceptions. Once you go to university you can't just slip back into the life you've had, you want more."

"If that's all you get, you might as well travel."

"You did, look what happened to you."

"Yeah, and?"

"What have you changed?"

"Nothing, I like my life the way it is."

"Don't you want more?"

"Not yet anyway. I've been thinking about stuff. You know. Did I make a mistake not going to college and all that, but I haven't really worked it out in my head yet."

"You can't keep doing what you're doing for the rest of your life."

"I don't intend to, but right now I don't know what I'm going to do instead of it. And you're starting to sound irritatingly like Mum."

"Well you know what they say about great minds."

Reach behind me and pull out my spliff case and pull out one.

"You got a light?"

"Yeah, but let me just open this window."

"Doesn't your mum know you're a smoker?"

"Listen, Tanya's baby was shock enough, me smoking would kill her."

"How's the baby?"

"Fine, and his name is Rashan. He crawls around and gets into everything."

"He's a baby, what do you expect?"

"He knows when you're coming as well. As soon as he hears the key in the door, he's looking to see who it is."

"Cute, aren't they?"

"'Cute' isn't the word you want to use when they've just been sick on you. And the shit? Eh! Makes me shudder to think about it."

Laugh as I pass her the joint and sit down at the table with her.

"I'm thinking about going for this job at this graphics place in Soho, what do you think?"

"Since when are you interested in graphics?"

"Since forever. Just because I did an English degree doesn't mean I can't be interested in anything else."

"What you thinking of doing for them?"

"I don't know, maybe write something, I'm not sure. Being on the dole for a while kicks the initiative out of you."

"Don't worry, just go for it, they might say yes."

"Then again, they might say no. Rejection isn't good."

"Don't know, never been rejected."

"Oh? What about Megan?"

"Eh! That was something else entirely."

"I'd call it rejection."

"Yeah, you're a girl, of course you'd call it that. I'd call it more a wait-and-see situation."

"It's been over a year."

"These things take time, you've got to let them take their course."

She shakes her head and hands back the spliff.

"So what you going to do now?"

"Sit here for a while, talk some more, try and figure out why women don't ask men out. You know, the usual."

"I've told you this already, women don't ask men out because we're afraid of rejection and because if we did, the men we approached would run a mile."

"I wouldn't."

"Yeah, and?"

"Yeah and what?"

"Just because you wouldn't doesn't mean most men wouldn't."

"Like that makes any difference."

I know London from couriering. But before I was a courier, I was a card-carrying vinyl junkie. I knew London through where the record shops were. If you asked me how to get somewhere I'd say, Yeah, that's near a record shop, went there a few times and brought the whole Roberta Flack back catalogue for a tenner. Or words to that effect. Buying records is like a religion: you are faithful to your god or suffer his wrath. And it is a vengeful god. No amount of praying or penance will get you back into its good books. The only way to stay faithful is to keep buying and buying lots of it. But with buying records, you get stigmatised with the anal German fuckers who can recite the ISDN bar code number off the back of every record they've ever brought. The dirty anorak brigade, whereupon visions of train spotters standing on a bridge in the middle of nowhere in the pouring rain, waiting for trains to come past, come to mind.

When you go into a club, you are prone to sharp waves of *deja vu* whenever a sample is heard as you stand still for several minutes trying to figure out where it came from and, once this task is performed, telling everyone in the club where it's from and on what album you can get it. Which can be very annoying. But I'm a junkie and I need my fix on a regular basis.

I skid up to the pavement and lock my bike up to a neighbouring lamp post. Stepping into the realms of vinyl. Vinyl Paradise, just off Berwick Street, is one of my regular haunts, but it's also close to those other places of delight for any junkie. Mr Bongo, Wild Pitch, Unity, Reckless Records, etc., etc., etc.

Step over to the counter and smile up at Steve, one of my old school friends. He's been working here as long as I've been buying records. His long hair tied back in a ponytail, which I keep telling him to get cut, but which he believes attracts the women. I think he thinks he's some sort of Samson.

"Anything new?"

"Nah, not much, we're waiting for our next shipment, should be in by Thursday."

"You busy?"

"No, not really."

He takes a quick look around, and except for the young kid at the front who's picking up flyers for his collection, it's a bit slow.

"I'm looking for this record, funk, but I don't know anything about it."

"Not good."

"It gets worse. I heard it last night for the first time in ten years and I can hum it to you."

Steve cocks his head to one side, as if to say, *I don't believe this*. I hum the first few bars of it and then sing what I can remember of the lyrics. Steve looks at me as if I'm speaking Italian.

"No good?"

"You must be joking. It's bad enough when people come in wanting some dub plate and start humming the bassline. At least I can pass them over to Eddie. But E, I never thought I'd see you doing it."

"I'm desperate, you don't know how desperate. I want that record. You wouldn't know anyone who'd know what it was?"

"I know a few people who are into the funk, I'll speak to them and give you a call. You still at the same number?"

"Yeah. Thanks."

I turn around and look at the interior, it's only on one floor and it stretches back a ways. On the opposite side of the shop are the ranks of records in their wire frames, with a growing collection of songs you can't afford to buy in plastic cases, mixed in with posters of various artists on the wall. Along the counter are three Technics decks, hooked up to headphones so that customers can listen before they buy. Just to make sure you understand. And at the very back, record bags, jackets and T-shirts for the very sad amongst us. Stand in front of the records and flick quickly through them. The action tried and true. Flick with my fingertips, pull it out if I think it's interesting before shoving it back and carrying on. You get quite efficient after a while, and you gain these lovely, roughened fingertips from constant searching. Steve's the master of the sticker sound bite. He spends ages coming up with shortened synopses and descriptions of the records to shove onto the outside covering.

TOP TUNE, BUY IT OR DIE. THE LIVING BASSLINE, ALL-TIME PARTY TUNE. BIGGIE SMALLS RARE DUB PLATE. You know, stuff like that. They make me smile whenever I see them. Steve's amusing himself by doing a little mixing.

"Where's Eddie?"

"Buying lunch, should be back soon. You got any fags?"

"Only spliffs."

"Oh go on then."

Pull out my case and light one up, taking a few quick tokes before handing it to him. Gives me a quick thumbs-up as he takes it before going back to his decks. I look around at the shop, waiting for the people to arrive and fill it. Making it a vinyl junky's heaven, rubbing shoulders with others of your kind. nudging them out of your way as you try to get to that record you saw over their shoulder. Waiting for them to finish with that rack of records so you can dive in and find what you want. Pulling out a whole load and going through them on the decks, listening to them. Putting some aside, discarding others. I come back to this space and time as Steve hands me back the spliff. Take another few quick tokes before giving it back. Steve looks surprised.

"Give me a ring when you've got those numbers."

"Yeah."

"I'll see you later."

"Yeah, later."

Side Two

August

Aaaaarrrgggh!

I'm sitting in Soho Square as is my want, munching on a focaccia sandwich from Benjy's over on Wardour Street. Bacon and chicken in a garlic mushroom sauce. Wash it down with a little water and belch rather loudly. Startling the pigeons strutting around my feet looking for crumbs.

"Pardon."

Crumple up the bag and bring my arm up as if I'm Jordan, snap my wrist and loop the bag skyward. Watching it arc gracefully towards the bin, hit its lip and fall onto the floor. Just not my day really. Get up and walk the few yards to the bin, picking up the crumpled bag and dropping it in. Turn back and sit on the bench, wondering how today could be so fucking slow. I've only done thirteen jobs in six hours. It's never been this slow. I've only done forty pounds worth of work. Which isn't good, not good at all. But what tops it all is that everyone else on circuit is doing 'nuff work. Every other call it's One Seven, or One Four, or One Nine. Every number except mine. Bastards.

I slip my Oakleys onto my forehead and lean back, looking up at the clouds drifting by. All fluffy and white. Remembering my date with Louise the week before. It was interesting, took her to that Italian place just off Cambridge Circus. Centrale, it's called, lovely atmosphere. The woman that runs the place was great, cracking jokes, courteous and concerned about the food. It was a shame to leave. But Louise was how I expected her, loud and brash, and into some strange mix of house and trance. We went to this club afterwards. I don't know what it was called, I've erased it from my memory. It was hellish. Just that continual thudding, raging through my brain. I could only stand up there and screw up my face.

Louise wanted to do a pill and was searching round forever looking for a dealer. I left her to it and sat by the bar sipping my spirits and getting mildly drunk as I smoked spliff after spliff. I saw Greer through the haze, all decked out in basically nothing, going at it like a nutter. If I haven't told you already, Greer's the living drugs baron, into everything and anything. Trips, Es, speed, mushrooms. When I first met him and was riding circuit with him, he'd come back from a night out on the razzle completely trashed and looking like death. Saying how he'd done a triple super dove, plus a bulldog and half a trip, and I'd ask him why. I'd never get any answer except that it was the best night he'd ever had. Well until the next one.

For the first time that night I slipped into the crush of the crowd, screwing every time someone would nudge me, shove their thumbs in my face or even grin in my direction. Until I got across the gap and shouted in Greer's ear to find out if he had any pills on him. It was a stupid question to ask, I know. But it had to be done, because Louise was starting to get on my nerves. I was starting to lose respect for myself that I was even checking for white girls. You know I don't want to become that nigga that only checks for white girls, because they lust after him, rather than trying for a black woman. I don't want to go down that road at all. But by the same token, I'm not going to just check one or the other. If I find you attractive I'm going to try and check you. As simple as that.

Greer had plenty of drugs on him, gave me two super doves and a microdot, which I dutifully took back to Louise, who had been starting to look downcast as her search for drugs was seeming to prove fruitless. She perked up plenty when she saw what was in my hand, and proceeded to dance all night with a frenzy I hadn't thought possible from her. Her breasts strapped tight to her chest by the tightness of the top that she was wearing. Her face flushed and her eyes bright, the pupils wide and open, even as the 30k light rig slashed across them.

She lives in North London, so we caught a cab. Pulling out into traffic with her body still moving to the music in her mind. The echoes of the thud still with her. Me sitting beside her, dying for a spliff to take the edge off the horror that is house. I've never liked house. Jungle is it for me, nothing else even comes close. Even though jungle and house have the same roots, all part of the rave scene, and to a certain extent, if house hadn't been done so well over here maybe jungle would never have been born. But it still makes no difference to me, house is still overrated, monotonous and just evil in all its many forms. It has no effect on me whatsoever, and wondering how people can enjoy listening to it gives me a headache. Thinking about this makes me wonder why I even went in the first place if I wasn't going to enjoy it. Well, I had to do something with Louise after dinner. She had wanted to go out, and I most probably would have traumatised her if I'd taken her to a jungle club. I don't think she's ready just yet. Who am I kidding? Louise will never be ready.

I'm very picky when it comes to women, and Louise is very attractive. But sometimes you just don't click; what more can be said really? If the sex is good, you might stretch it out for a few weeks, but in the end it's just another one that you chalk up to experience.

Look around, nothing much happing. The rush of people that were here for the lunchtime struggle has tapered off and all that's left is tourists, couriers and winos. Play with my radio for a few minutes just to check whether it's still working.

Play with the volume, before letting it lie on top of my bag. Put my bag at the head of the bench and lie down. Turn the volume down because it's closer to my ear. Stick my hand out and grab onto my frame and close my eyes. Letting the sun beat down on me and take me into slumber land.

"One one, one one."

I wake slowly, a sticky tacky feeling in my mouth. Everything's slow as if I'm moving through Jello. Look up and reach above me to grab the radio and reply.

"One one, one one."

"One one, Westons on Jermyn Street, going W1."

"Roger roge."

I sit up and rub the sleep out of my eye. Look down at my watch to see how long I've been asleep. Forty-five minutes. Shit! Pull out my sheets and write down the new job. Before stretching strong and getting that familiar cracking in my chest. Blink continually to wake myself up, grab my bike and push it out of the square before jumping on outside the gate and ducking out into traffic. Straighten my bag and I'm diving through traffic at a rate of knots. When you haven't been doing anything for a while, any job you get you want to do it quickly in the hopes that another one comes on you fast.

I head down Oxford Street towards Oxford Circus, taking a slightly longer route, but I feel I need it just to get me back into the swing of things. Duck out behind a bus and take a sweeping left onto Regent Street. Don't pull the brakes as I fly through pedestrians trying to cross the road. Cut through the traffic stuffed up along the road, shoving the bike through gaps that continually get smaller. Jump lights continually looking for coppers. That crackdown is still going on and I don't really want to try and outrun one of them.

Round Piccadilly Circus, then down the Haymarket, not stopping for breath anywhere. Pull a hard right to take me over to Lower Regent Street, then up the hill, banking across four lanes of traffic to get over to Jermyn Street. Find the right number as I pedal slowly along the curb. Stopping every now and then to let pedestrians past. Can't see any lampposts or parking meters to chain to, so I bring it in after I buzz and leave her sitting forlornly in the corridor.

Up the steps and into the reception area. Putting on my brightest smile for the very young receptionist.

"I've come to collect a package, going to W1."

She hands it over and I put it into my bag as I skip down the stairs.

"One one, one one."

"One one, one one."

"One one, one one, POB."

"Roger roge, knock it out."

"Roger."

Climb back on board and dart out, jumping the kerb as I do a small wheelie away and into traffic. Not bothering to glance back at the pedestrians who do a double-take as I move away. I ride hard, knowing where I'm going. Slice through traffic, taking a few risks here and there and generally just going like a nutter. Look over my shoulder, go left round a slowing van and then inside, the driver slowing down in his rented car in front of him. Break hard, bouncing my back wheel, change a few gears as I come to a set of lights. Move forward till I can see the lights for the traffic coming across me and wait for them to change from green to red. Jump across as they turn amber and pull out some space between me and the cars following, swing over to the left-hand side and brush past someone walking in the road. Change two gears and turn the gear hard. Get out of the second for an instant as I cut between two moving lorries, ducking my head underneath the wing mirror. Hearing my bag's strap slap the door. Look for the door and slash over, pulling a massive skid, whipping the back end round as I hit the kerb and jump off.

Wipe the sweat from my brow and lock up. A smile creasing my face at the familiar feeling of adrenalin pumping through my body at having ridden hard. Pull the package out and drop it on the security guard's desk. He looks at me as I pull out my sheet and ask him for his signature.

"Could you sign your name and print it here?"

He looks down at the sheet and fumbles for his pen before asking, "Where do I sign? Oh right, I got you."

I look heavenward and bite my lip and marvel at the attention span of the London security guard. Pull the sheet out of his hand and walk out of the revolving doors.

"One one, one one."

"One one, one one."

"One one, empty W1."

"Roger roge, come back towards me."

"Roger."

I unlock my bike and make the decision to ride hard back towards the city. Click my foot into the pedals and tear off into traffic, which is getting heavy as rush hour approaches, people trying to get stuff done before they are bogged down in the molasses which is rush hour. Stick the bike into a sweeping left turn and then down a slight hill, looking far in front of me to make sure nothing untoward happens. Change gear as I feel myself start to spin out, before lowering my head and trying to make myself more aerodynamic.

See the E-type, pull up to my left and ignore it, shifting

slightly over to my right. Look right to check there's nothing close beside me. Look back and I'm flying.

Feel the bike come with me. My feet haven't broken free of my spds. The wind's snapped out of me and I can feel the bruising beginning on my chest. Everything's slowed. I'm sailing through the air. I can feel the wind moving through all of the shortened hairs on my cheeks. Feel the direction in which they're moving. Smell the perfume of the woman pushing her baby on the other side of the street. The heavy smell of petrol coming from exhausts. See the concrete coming closer. Every crack and depression in it is highlighted and I can hear my brain telling me this is going to hurt.

No time to do anything, even though time has stood still. If I wanted, I could do anything. My head twists and I see the white Jaguar, can look into the eyes of the driver as he sits there hunched forwards. Mobile phone by his ear, his other hand on the steering wheel. His eyes are blue, pale and light. He's got an expensive haircut, his hair swept away from his face, and a big gold ring on his forefinger. See my reflection in the wire-rimmed wheels. My Oakleys covering my eyes, so I can't see whether I look scared or not. Wonder why I can't hear anything but the wind whistling past me, even though my reflection's got its mouth open in a scream.

I hit the floor hard, feel the impact in my shoulder and side. Everything goes numb along the side that I hit the floor with. Withering pain shooting up my arm. Then shit goes black.

Payback's A Bitch

I wake up and I don't know how long I've been out for. The first thing into my mind is this is what Danny would have woken up to. Since Danny died, I think it every time I've had a crash where I've been knocked unconscious. And there have been a few. Three at the last count. Two of those did serious damage, the other I was just bruised.

I can hear the voices. All of them sounding concerned. They start out as just a loud rumble, then slowly clarify into separate voices and words. Struggle upwards as I open my eyes and see them leaning over me. Some woman starts talking to me.

"Lie still, we've called the ambulance and they should be on their way. Just lie still."

My eyes brush over her as I pull myself to a seated position, not taking any notice of what she's saying. She don't know what she's talking about. She's probably her office's first aider or some other bollocks. Start to stand and grab a hand to help me to my feet. Already my body's starting to hurt all over. But nothing's numb, which is good. Shows I haven't broken anything. I get to my feet and stagger, falling into someone while I hold my arm against my side. Getting spots at the sides of my vision, must be the rush of blood to my head.

Turn around and the crowd's quite big, at least twenty people. I'm surprised. Look around for my bike. Push through the crowd. I remember still being clipped in when I went over the car.

"Where's my bike?"

I'm surprised by the hoarseness of my voice, as if I haven't drunk for a few days or I've just undergone an operation. Someone points and I make my way through the crowd in the direction that their finger was pointing in.

"It came off when you hit the floor, so we put it over on the pavement."

The crowd parts and I feel like crying when I see her.

She's fucked, totally and utterly. Just like that Bear Valley I had. The front wheel's buckled severely. Front forks bent back at a ridiculous angle. The frame's snapped and my handlebars are bent almost in two. I try to bend down, but pain flares up in my knee and I have to fight not to shout out. I concede by letting out a rush of air.

Turn around with murder in my heart.

"Where's the fucker that pulled out in front of me?"

I look round, fierce. Trying to make him out in the crowd.

"Did you see where he went?"

I can't see him. Those blue eyes aren't in the crowd. Hobble over to the road he pulled out of and his car's not there. Have to breathe deep to stop myself from screaming. The woman who told me to lie down steps forward with something white and flimsy in her hand.

"He left this, said he was in a hurry. He told me to tell you to phone him as soon as you're recovered to sort everything out."

I snatch the card out of her hand. It's a business card for

Jason Milson
A&R Director
Zefal Music

I know them, one of the major labels, up there with Sony,

RCA/BMG, Virgin, Polydor and the rest. All the stuff that you get on vinyl from them is really shoddy, just like Giant. My eyes burn into the numbers on the bottom as I haul myself over to a phone box and search through my pockets for some change. I struggle for a second trying to stand upright as well as use the phone, as my leg is becoming increasingly truculent about having any weight put on it. I dig out the coins and punch in the number for his mobile. I get that trite fucking message about how "the mobile phone that you have called is unavailable, please try again later."

I slam down the phone and shove in some more coins and phone the office number.

"Hello, Zefal Music."

"Can I speak to Jason Milson?"

"I'll just put you through."

I'm tight-lipped, biting out the words as my body starts sending all sorts of pain messages to my brain.

"Hello, Jason Milson's office."

"Can I speak to Jason please?"

"I'm sorry, he's not in at the moment, can I take a message?"

"Yes, you can. Tell him this is the courier that he knocked off his bike today and when I get him I'm going to fuck him up seriously."

"Excuse me?"

"Just tell him, he'll understand."

I slam down the telephone, feeling the anger stuck in my chest. Pick up the phone and start to slam it against the receiver. Again and again and again and again. while the voyeurs stand around the telephone box and watch me.

I sit in front of the TV in my room, my eyes glazed over with a rapidly defrosting pack of peas on my knee. Iago had to come and get me from A&E and drive me home. The crash didn't do any serious damage, just a lot of bruising. The way my knee feels, I'm surprised I haven't torn any ligaments or anything. Just sitting here flicking through the channels. Mum went through the roof when I told her, but there was nothing she could do anyway. The remains of my bike are in some police lot somewhere, I'll have to go and get her soon. So that I can mourn her passing properly. Had to call in from hospital and tell them that I'd be off the circuit for a while. Waiting for all this bruising to go down and trying to get some money together to buy a new bike. Last week's money should be coming through, so that should tide me over for a week or two.

Pick up my phone and then put it down again. I don't really feel like talking. The only person I want to talk to is unavailable. I pick up the card for the godknowshowmanyeth time and stare at the numbers on it. I've committed them to memory.

I can't even get out of bed to put some records on, my body hurts all over. Some more bumps and bruises and scars to add to my collection. Look down at my heavily strapped knee and try and figure out how I'm going to get to the freezer to change this bag of peas for a new one so hopefully the swelling will go down as quickly as possible. So I will be able to walk without the crutches they gave me.

I flick numbly through the channels, my eyes seeing but not seeing, and leave it on some cartoon. Grit my teeth and try to move, but the pain forces tears to my eyes, so I sit back down and pick up the phone. Stabbing the numbers with my finger, hoping my anger will travel down the line and bring an answer. Put it to my ear and find it's ringing.

"Hello."

"Can I speak to Jason Milson?"

"Speaking."

My heart leaps with a ferocious joy as I achieve success. Wonder what I'm going to say. Should I swear, curse the man down the line, or should I be smooth and calm? Fuck it.

"My names Eder O'niah, I'm the guy you took off his bike today while you were talking on your mobile phone you fuckwit."

"Oh!"

"That's all you've got to say for yourself, you bastard? You took me to the fucking kerb and then drove off. Last time I heard, the police were well interested in your whereabouts."

"Look, I'm really sorry, it was all my fault, I wasn't looking. But I had to get to a meeting…"

"Fuck your meeting, and fuck you being sorry, what are you going to do about me? You've fucked my knee, you fucked my bike. How am I supposed to live? To eat? Where's the money going to be coming from? Eh! Eh!"

"Look, can we arrange a meeting to discuss this?"

"Yeah, we can arrange a meeting just as soon as I can walk with these crutches."

"Shit! I didn't think it was that bad."

"Since you weren't the person who kissed concrete at thirty miles per hour, you can't be saying fuck all."

"Look, I'll come round now if it'll make you feel any better?"

"No, what would make me feel any better would be being able to walk. That's not possible, so I'd advise you to bring a truckload of money with you, otherwise you'll be seeing me in court."

"What's your address?"

I give it to him and slam down the phone. Happy within myself that things have started rolling. Trying to tot up figures in my head about how much money I should be expecting to get. I'll discuss it with Mum when she gets back. I've had quite useful sums of money before. Usually the threat of court action is enough and they get their insurance to cough up quickly. The money usually takes time to come through, which is a bit of a bastard, but then again, beggars can't be choosers.

I hear the key in the door and Mum comes through. Home early from work to see how her son's doing. She shoves her head round the door and just looks at me. She's been here before, and even though she wants to show me some sympathy, I know that she's still angry. I can tell by that glint in her eye and the way that her eyes are slightly red from where she's been crying.

"I told you to buy a helmet" is all she says before she leaves. Letting the door swing shut gently behind her. I can hear her in the kitchen starting to prepare something. My door opens a few minutes later as she chucks me a new bag of frozen peas.

"Thanks."

I chuck her back the one that I've just been using and try not to cry when I shift my leg to put the new one on. The knee throbs and bucks every time I try to move it, so I just leave it. The doctor said to be off it for about a week to ten days and just keep the swelling down, keeping it higher than my heart. But he wouldn't tell me when I'd be able to ride again, or if I should even ride again. So I sit and wait for that bastard to arrive and see what he has to say for himself.

It's getting dark when Khadija rings, her voice soft with concern on the other side of the phone.

"I heard you came off again, what happened?"

"Some bastard came out in front of me and I went over

the bonnet. I didn't do any real damage, just knocked myself unconscious and bruised everything."

"How are you doing? Do you want me to come round?"

"No, I'm fine. I've given him a ring and he said he's going to come round to sort stuff out, so maybe I might be able to stick him for some cash."

"You think so?"

"You never know. If he doesn't pay right away, his insurance will, loss of earnings and all that."

"Yeah, well if you say so."

"Don't be so down-hearted, it'll turn out alright."

The doorbell goes and I stiffen as I have since he said he'd be round, thinking that everyone at the door was him. I hear the door open, but what is said is muffled, then his head pops round the door.

"I've got to go."

"Okay, I'll speak to you later."

"Yeah."

I put the phone down and watch him step carefully into my room, trying not to step on anything or make a mess. Watch him dressed in his jeans and T-shirt.

"Can I sit down?"

"Only if you brought your checkbook with you?"

He stiffens as if I've shot him. His head snapping up and his brow furrowing.

He sits opposite me, by my decks, looking round at them, my records, out my window, but not directly at me.

"Nice place you've got here."

I let him stew for a few seconds.

"That's a nice collection of records you've got there."

"Really?"

"How long have you been buying records?"

"Since I was in school"

"I'm really sorry about the accident. It was totally my fault. I was busy on the phone and I wasn't paying attention to where I was going."

"You don't have to tell me, I know."

"I don't really want to get my insurance people involved in this."

"Why, you weren't drinking as well, were you?"

"No."

"Damn."

"Look, I'm really sorry."

"Being sorry don't make it any easier that you fucked me over and then didn't even have the courtesy to see if I was alright."

He lowers his head, as if I'm his mum and have just told him not to swear in church.

"So what are you going to do?"

"I…"

"Well, for a start you're going to shell out for a new bike, because mine's been fucked. As you know."

He lowers his head again.

"I'm really—"

"Sorry, yeah, I know!"

He looks around to get away from looking at me.

"A new bike's going to cost you two grand at least."

"Two thousand pounds?"

He looks shocked.

"Yeah, two grand. Then of course there's compensation for time off work. Loss of earnings, you know. At three hundred a week, maybe six weeks off work, that's 1800, round that up to two grand."

"Hold on a minute."

"No you hold on. Just 'cause you got a Jag don't mean you can be taking people to the kerb. You've got a responsibility."

"I know, I know."

"Well if you know, what are you bitching for?"

He looks around again, looking for a way out.

"Look, are you a DJ?"

"Yeah, when I'm not couriering."

"Good, then if you want to, rather than offering you money, I'd like to offer you a job as an A&R man at the label I work for."

"Why? When all you have to do is give me a lump sum of about six grand and I'll be out of your hair forever?"

"Because I'm really truly sorry about what happened."

"Yeah, right."

"And a vacancy has just come up. You're a DJ, you know the club scene, things could happen."

"Yeah, like this. You're taking the piss aren't you?"

"No, I'm being dead serious. Look, you'll be starting on twelve grand a year. If you like it and are any good at it you could go to twenty, twenty-five easy."

I'm mentally calculating how much twelve grand a year works out to per week. Something like 220, I think, if my maths is any good.

"So what do you say?"

I think for a second. If worse comes to worst, I can always duck out with some freebies. And if my knee heals properly, as I think it's going to, couriering awaits.

"Okay."

"Great, well give me a ring when you're feeling better and I'll sort everything out with our people."

And he's out the door like a scared rabbit, his conscience salved by the offering of a job.

Artists & Repertoire

The building's big, slap right in the centre of town, not more than five minutes away from the Sony building on Great Marlborough Street. This slashing steel and concrete thing high in the sky. Well not that high, about seven stories. I look up at it and look down on the names I've got scribbled on the back of Jason's card. I didn't know what to wear, so I put on some jeans and my Timberlands, a faded old T-shirt and my worn jean jacket. I also borrowed an old wooden cane from Khadija that her father used to use when his gout got bad. It's coming in very handy as my knee is starting to play up. Look down at my watch. I was told to get here at about half ten, since A&Rs don't get in till about eleven as they've been out on the razzle the night before. Push my way through the revolving doors and walk stiffly over to the receptionist's desk, which is set in this massive marble floor with a design in it. Hearing the click of my cane as I walk across it. Sunlight's pouring in from the space down the centre which is open to the sky. I lean back and look up through the buildings and watch a jumbo jet pass by. Look down and see the receptionist looking at me, with her Janet Jackson hands-free headset on her head.

"I'm here to see Jason Milson."

"Who should I say is calling?"

"Eder O'niah"

She looks at me strange and I wink for her. I stand by the desk for a second before moving over to the leather settees, set in a semi-circle against the wall and surrounded by plants. I sit and feel my knee creak uneasily. The swelling's gone down, but the stiffness and the pain are still there. Which is why I'm taking the living painkillers. The doctor seems to feel I might need physiotherapy, just to make the healing process go a little faster. I just wanted to know whether I can have sex with it in this condition. All the rest of my bumps and bruises have turned a nasty puss yellow from their equally evil pitch black. The whole of my right side is covered with them and I haven't undressed in front of a girl since the accident. For one, it's too uncomfortable, and for three, I look like Mr Burns with all of these bruises. It's just disgusting.

"Mr Milson will see you now."

I lever myself out of the deep seat using the cane and the arm of the chair, trying not to bend my knee or shout out in pain. I manage to do it, but not without a struggle, and then I've got to walk across the floor to collect some sort of silly visitor's pass. It feels weird coming through the front doors of a building. As a courier you usually get sent round the back like a nigga to hand your package to some security guard. I try not to look too uncomfortable taking the pass from her.

"Little rugby accident."

She nods her head in sympathy.

"Mr Milson is on the fourth floor."

"Thanks."

I walk-cum-limp over to the lift, leaning heavily on my cane, and wait for it to come down. The lights signal its arrival, and it's one of those glass-fronted fuckers where you can look all the way down as you travel up, with a door on both sides to let you out into the office space. I put my forehead against the glass and stare downwards at the rapidly receding floor as the lift takes me up to see Jason. Smile at the thought of someone with a Jheri curl getting their head up against the glass. A bell goes off and the doors behind me open up.

I limp out into an open-plan office with lots of desks stretching away. Along the sides of the space are more conventional offices, with doors opening onto this communal workplace. All of the offices along the sides have huge glass windows, letting in a huge wave of light. I limp slowly down, looking at all the fresh young things moving swiftly about through the tables and potted plants. Every door has record stickers on them for various acts, and posters are up on the wall. Macs are sitting on tables with tapes just strewn around. Reminding me of Iago's car. I see Jason come out of a door down at the end and walk slowly towards him. He sees me and a smile comes across his smooth features. I still haven't forgiven him for kicking me to the kerb, but we've talked a lot lately and we seem to have a lot in common, except for the fact that he's nine years older and is on a hundred and fifty grand a year, with it expected to go to a quarter of a million soon.

He stretches out his hand and I have to shift hands on my stick to shake it.

"How you been?"

"Not too bad, not too bad."

"Good, come on let me show you who you'll be working with."

I walk behind him stiffly, trying to keep up, but not about to put myself to the sword for personal vanity. We arrive at a sweeping circular attachment at the end of the office space, which is just all glass. It's like looking over a precipice. The far wall, or where the far wall should be, is just a curved clear window looking out over London. I wonder how they ever do any work here, but keep that thought to myself. Sitting around the tables which hold together the centre of the space are five people. Jason introduces me to them one at a time.

"This is Ronald Davies, he's our manager."

A tall man with hard features, sharp eyes and heavy eyebrows. His hands thick and heavy like an anchor.

"Joel Mcelroy, a scout like you."

Small with a round face, bright-red cheeks and an infectious smile. I try not to laugh as I imagine him and the other elves running through the forest, red hair on fire.

"Janey Crawford, also a scout like you."

She's nice but her chin looks a bit weak and she hasn't lost all of her puppy fat. Brown hair brushed away from her forehead.

"Simone Wilson, another scout."

I look at her and feel attracted instantly. Dark hair and dark skin, she looks very Mediterranean. But her eyes are cold and distracted. She looks bored, with work, with life.

"And last but not least, Michael Ryan, who is our regional scout. He's usually out and about, but I thought he should meet you."

He's good, I like him already, ready smile and a huge mop of uncombed blonde hair, which has sort of turned into an Afro.

"This is Eder O'niah, the latest recruit to our happy voyage across the seas of A&R."

I wave my hand at everyone and try to remove the discomfort from my knee by putting my weight on my other leg.

"Hi."

"Don't worry, they'll show you the ropes. I'll leave you to it."

Jason ducks out behind me, moving over to his office, to do what, I don't know, and I'm left with a group of people that I don't know, doing a job that I have no understanding of whatsoever. If I'm supposed to be finding new talent, what am I doing sitting in an office? Look around at the various sets sitting on shelves. Most of them aren't worthy of the name hi-fi, most are just midi systems made by Akai or Sanyo. Just cheap bollock rubbish. My gaze swings back to the group, who have split and moved off to various phones around the office. Ronald is the only one watching me. I move slowly over and sit down beside him.

"So, Ronald, what happens now?"

"I'll get Joel to take you through what happens in a day and bring you up to speed."

"Okay."

He gets up and moves away from me, stepping round to his own little office space, leaving us plebs to the light and sun of the communal working space. Lean back in my chair and stretch out my leg. Just to ease the slight cramp in it. Bend to it and massage it gently. Rubbing with my thumb around the knee area, and then moving up to my thigh. Joel comes round and slaps me gently on the shoulder.

"Don't mind Ron, he's like that with everyone."

"Like what?"

"A bit short, he's got a bit of a temper on him. I don't think he handles pressure very well."

"Maybe he should think about another job then."

"No, no, he loves the job, he's just not very good with people."

I look at him and raise my eyebrows, something I learned from Khadija to lend an air of incredulousness to whatever has been said before.

"Well, I might as well ask this now, how did you get this job?"

"Jason knocked me off my bike about a week ago, came round to my house, saw I was a DJ and said, How would you like to be an A&R man getting twelve grand a year? and I said okay. Here I am. I wouldn't advise it for everyone."

Joel looks at me strangely, then nods his head.

"Yeah, alright, you're joking, right?"

"No. That's why I've got the cane, so I can walk without falling over constantly."

Now I seem to have not only Joel's attention but everyone else's. The voices that I heard chatting away on the phone, have stopped to listen to what I'm saying to Joel.

"Jason knocked you off your bike?"

"Yeah, the idiot was speaking on his mobile phone and pulled out into the main road when I was licking speed towards him. Went over the front of his bonnet. Haven't any of you wondered why he hasn't been driving his Jag lately?"

Swivel in the chair and look at the bemused faces, lift my hands up to the air in mock frustration and turn back to Joel.

"So what do I do around here? Give me a breakdown."

"Well, we answer phone calls, listen to demo tapes that get sent in, speak to managers, new ones, old ones, we arrange meetings with managers and artists, arrange studio time, visit studios to see how artists are doing. Sometimes we go to showcases in the afternoon, visit independent record labels. Then in the evenings we go to gigs, pubs and clubs, etc., and see what's new, what's happening, what's hot and try and sign it. That's basically it."

"Sounds like a lot of fun."

I rub my forehead slowly and wonder what I've got myself into.

"What music do you listen to?"

Look up at Simone standing over me, flicking her hair out of her eyes.

"Hip hop, swing, rare groove, funk, jazz funk, jungle, that's about it really."

"You like jungle?"

"Don't you?"

"No."

"You're missing out on a lot. I'll bring some in and you can listen to… actually…"

Lever myself out of the chair and quickly hobble over to the midi system and turn it on, look carefully for a few seconds as I search for the tuner button, then another few seconds looking for how to change stations, before running through the dial looking for a pirate station, Kool FM or Girls or Eruption. Swing swiftly through the dial and find one, just beyond Kiss. Hear the bassline coming through and the MC chatting swiftly over the top, patois-laden poetry moving in time with the bassline. The running staccato drum pattern broken up and jagged over the top. Whip up the bass and turn up the volume some more. Hear the cheap speakers making a noise they shouldn't but ignore it. Look at the other scouts as they look blankly at me.

"This is jungle."

They just stare, no expression, then out of my eye I see Ronald shove his head out of his door.

"Turn that down, people trying to work here."

Shrug and lower the volume.

"Shit, you well behind here."

I hobble back over to my chair.

"Okay, so what music you into? Simone first."

"I'm into house, hard house, techno, a bit of acid jazz, stuff like that."

"Janey?"

"Me, I'm more into indies, like Elastica, Sleeper, Oasis, Blur. Brit pop I suppose you could call it. Echobelly as well, a lot of people really."

"Joel?"

"I'm more of a funk person, but I like a lot of indie stuff as well. But I'm well into trip hop, Mo wax, Portishead, Massive, Tricky, that sort of sound."

"Shit, we do have a mixed bag here. So everybody's into different stuff, but what do you sign? Who do you sign? Have any of you signed anyone?"

"Well that's a bit different. We're just scouts so we don't really sign any acts. Well, we can, but if we do it's like one a year or so, because when you sign an act they become your responsibility."

"All I want to know is what have we signed recently? You know. I know who you've got on your American roster of acts because I've brought most of their records, but I have no idea who you've got signed over here. If anyone."

Joel looks at his watch, quickly checking what time it is.

"Well, I've got to see this new act we're developing, all-girl singing group called Innuendo. They're getting some press shots done at the minute."

"We're talking a pop group here, aren't we?"

"Yeah, we're hoping top twenty."

I close my eyes and hope it doesn't get any worse. Trying to figure out what I can do within this system of work. They don't seem to have any interest in the music that I enjoy, and I haven't seen or heard of anyone in the UK that they've signed that I know of. This girlie combo thing doesn't exactly fill me with confidence either. More than likely just another Eternal or something, or even worse a Shampoo. Argggggghhh.

"They're at a studio right now, you can come with me if you want. Have a look at them?"

"Yeah, why not, I don't think I'm an office sort of person."

"Great, I'll just call a cab."

The studio's in North London, just off the City Road, some old factory that's been renovated into studio and office spaces. I'm worried as soon as I see it looming into the sky. My mind already working out how much pain I'm going to put myself through even through the happy glaze of the painkillers as I pull myself up the stairs. I'm praying for a lift. It's all I can do. Just pray as Joel pops out. The black cab moving off into the distance, heat haze shimmering there out in front of it.

I follow Joel into the building, aware of the coolness of it in relation to the heat outside. And thank god as we walk up to a very big, very wide lift. One of those old ones with the two sliding doors. It takes us up to the sixth floor, right to the top. Where we walk down a long white corridor, with light pouring in from the windows beside our faces. Stop outside a door which has a nice design and the name Rebellion Photography underneath. Joel knocks then pushes on the door and steps into the darkness inside. We move into a very big space, which is pitch black except for a bank of lights on the other side, where three girls, not more than sixteen, maybe seventeen, with a fan blowing their hair, are pouting and posing in front of a camera as a huge flash keeps going off. A voice, clipped, but soft and husky, with a very faint edge of a Jamaican accent, tells the girls to "move your hair more. Toss you head, stick out your tits. Your goddesses, here to make men desire you."

We walk across, Joel whispering in my ear about his band.

"They're my baby, I signed them a couple of months ago,

they're my first signing, so I'm hoping they do really well. But sometimes it takes a bit of time. You know, getting the marketing men to part with some cash to promote them properly, that sort of thing. But you'll find that out for yourself, when you try to get something off the ground."

Turn my head and lose the rest of what he's saying as I look at his baby. The girls seem to be very mature, if that be the word. Desirable in many ways. Firm moulded bodies and high pert breasts. Their faces, while not exactly model beautiful, are attractive and interesting. They are multi-racial, one black, one Asian and one white, Mediterranean looking. Capturing the innocence and knowledge of the age group that they are a part of. My attention drifts from them to the person behind the camera. The voice makes it out to be a woman, but I have no idea of the face or figure of her as she crouches over the camera, her eye to the viewfinder.

I stand with Joel on the edge of the light and wait for the session to be finished. I look around for somewhere to sit and see a settee on the other side of the room, the side which we came from. Next to it is a kitchen space with a gas cooker and a tall fridge freezer, some cupboards and work surfaces. I walk over and edge myself carefully into the chair while Joel still stands, eager to get in and see how his girls are doing. Close my eyes and let the pain wash through me. The painkillers digging into my side as they rest in my pocket. I feel to take a few more to try and blunt the rising pain, but decide against it. I want to be totally cognizant and not weighed down mentally by the drugs. The only reason I've got the painkillers on me is because I didn't know how the people I would be working with would take to me smoking weed in their presence. When

I'm at home I smoke weed to blunt the pain, as I trust it rather than the painkillers.

The shooting stops and the lights come slowly up, and I see a photographic assistant standing beside the camera with some film in his hand and a black box which looks like a remote control. Maybe that's what he's using to turn up the lights. Look up to the ceiling and see the lights that are up there, a series of three rows of three, slowly lowering to just above head height and lighting the white studio evenly.

The photographer steps back from her camera, letting her assistant take out film and change magazines while she runs her hand through her short hair. Her olive skin glowing as if she's been on holiday and come back with a tan. She turns and looks at Joel, smiling slightly in recognition, and I see it's the light-skin girl from the club. She's dressed in dungarees over a T-shirt, with some sandals on her feet. Some of those Nike bastards, but she looks good, with a thick gold bangle tight against her right bicep. She looks in my direction and I don't know whether she recognises me or not.

The girls, as if suddenly given new life, bounce away from their positions in front of the camera, start talking loudly, voices rising ever higher, laughing and joking amongst themselves. Music comes from nowhere and my head turns repeatedly as I try to see where the speakers are and what they are. Some dub, deep bassline, and a weird collection of instruments over the top. A sitar and a violin sift through each other and create a discordant but strangely haunting sound. The girls start to dance, moving hips in a sexual way, making me pine for the darkness and smoky claustrophobia of a dance, with hips rubbing against mine and people flashing lighters. I want to be with them, but they are caught up in their own enjoyment, and my knee at the moment isn't the most conducive to rapid movement of any kind.

Joel moves over to his girls and stands and talks to them as they stop dancing for a second to listen to him. He gestures expansively with his hands and they nod. But I'm more concerned with the photographer. I have nowhere to go. Stuck between a rock and a hard place. I wonder whether she recognises me, and if she does, will she say anything? Then again, I recognise her and I still want her. Just because I made a complete ass of myself the first time doesn't mean the desire for her has disappeared. I look at her and conclude that she looks better with her hair short. She looks older, more sophisticated. Now, with her hair cut short at the back and long wisps of hair framing her face, she looks more secure in herself, more confident than she did at the club or at the shop. She leaves her camera equipment and walks towards me. I'm not sure whether she's coming over to me or the kitchen. My stomach starts to roll nervously. Try to let it settle by thinking about the pain in my knee. Then, as I see the T-shirt that she is wearing is really a halter top, and that through the big gaps in her dungaree sides I can see the soft skin of her stomach and her hips, covered by big Calvin Klein briefs pulled up high to her waist, I feel a surge of desire.

She walks up to me.

"Hi."

Then past and into the kitchen, opening the fridge and pulling out a can of Coke.

"Would you like something to drink?"

"Orange juice if you've got it."

Hear her fiddling about in the kitchen, not wanting to twist around to see what she's doing. A glass of orange juice appears in front of my face, I take it.

"Thanks"

She stands in front of me sipping from her Coke, looking down at me with her head turned to one side. Her eyes looking at me quizzically.

"Do I know you?"

Wonder what to say, what to do, who to be.

"We met briefly at a club a few weeks back. You had your hair longer then. I came up to you to say something when I lost it and left you standing there. Then there was a fire, the sprinklers came on and everyone left."

Her face lights up with the recognition of what happened.

"Oh yeah, I remember now. I was wondering what you were doing. Why didn't you say anything?"

"It's a long and embarrassing story which I'd rather not tell."

"Oh!"

"Yes, oh!"

She takes another sip of her Coke and I watch her lips as she drinks. How her eyes close as her head tilts back, the lovely curve of her neck, and I want her. I want to bury my mouth against her neck and suck on it, bringing up red marks there, making her hand come up and hold the back of my neck, pushing my mouth closer to her flesh.

"Er, what did you say?"

"I said we haven't been introduced yet. I'm Inez Kertin."

"Eder O'niah."

"That's a strange name."

"I could say the same about you, you don't look Spanish."

"My father's Jamaican, he called me Inez after a close friend he met while he was on tour."

"That doesn't explain the fact that you've got Chinese eyes."

"My mother's Cantonese, from Hong Kong, she met my

father while he was touring the Far East. So give me the low down on your heritage, Mr O'niah."

"The surname's Irish, though my grandmother is Scottish, my mother has a Jamaican father, and my father is from Barbados. My first name is of my own choosing, I was christened Alexander Liam, but I call myself Eder, after a Brazilian football player."

"Hmmm!"

"Exciting, isn't it?"

She looks up as her assistant calls out her name.

"I'll be back in a second."

"Don't worry, I'm not going anywhere."

She looks at me while I raise my eyebrows in answer to her unasked question. She smiles a small smile and walks away as I watch her buttocks move within the bagginess of her dungarees. I want her even more now than before. Find myself thinking that that was easy and painless. Has she got a boyfriend? And how old is she? Old enough to have experience, or just someone with an exotic heritage?

Joel strolls over to me and I watch him with his rather self-conscious gait. I don't think that being in this industry suits him. He looks too naive and innocent, and I get the feeling that it'll chew him up and spit him out.

"The girls are doing fine. They were a bit nervous at first. But they're really getting into it. Can't wait to do some more."

"Can they sing?"

"Of course, why do you ask?"

"Just wondered. So what happens now?"

"Well their manager should be here in a little while and I'll speak to him and try to iron out any problems he's got. After that it's back to the office and a showcase about three."

Look over to the far side of the studio and watch Inez

speaking to her assistant, holding some shots in her hand. Wonder how she got them so quickly and try to figure out where her darkroom is. She points ahead of her, giving him instructions. He nods and then moves away to the lights that were illuminating the girls. Turning them off and moving them around. The girls start to sing, harmonising, their voices rising and falling with an angel-like quality as they meld seamlessly into the music. Joel looks at me as I raise my eyebrows.

"Good, aren't they?"

"Better than I expected."

I forget Joel as Inez walks over towards us, the photos still in her hand. She reaches us and Joel gives her a small hug.

"How are they?"

"They're great, really easy to work with."

Joel turns as if he's left me out.

"Eder this is Inez, I don't know whether you two introduced yourselves to each other earlier."

"We did."

"Inez is a friend from school, we both went to Holland Park."

"Oh."

"It's a school for the young, rich and foreign."

"I see."

"What Joel means is the children of the rich and foreign."

"Any good?"

"If you can speak a lot of different languages, yes."

"I got Inez this job, got to get as many of your friends into the industry as possible."

"I was the only photographer you knew who wouldn't force you to pay huge amounts of money for my services."

"Well there's that as well. I'm going to speak with my act, give me a shout when you're ready."

Joel walks away as Inez hands me the small photos. They're Polaroids, black and white, showing the girls, provocative and strangely innocent as well, bringing out the childish qualities of them.

"What do you think?"

"They're nice."

"I'm holding an exhibition in a few days' time, would you like to come?"

"Is that like a date?"

"That depends."

"On what?"

"On whether you're in a relationship or not?"

"You know, you are the first woman who has ever asked me out."

"I get the feeling that I'm not."

"You are, and I will come to your exhibition. What are the photos of?"

"Wait and see."

"You're not one of those secretive women, are you? You know, the kind that like to keep stuff about themselves secret so they have new stuff to throw at you to put spice into the relationship."

"No, I'm not. I just want to see your reaction to it."

"Oh!"

Joel calls out for her and her neck twists and I want to bite it. I want to be amazingly sexual and graphic. I want to ask her what she would sound like if I was inside her and throbbing.

She looks back and pulls a postcard from her back pocket.

"Here."

It's a postcard with the word "Mysteries" in white on a plane black background, and on the back are the details of where the exhibition is to be held.

"Thanks"

"I'll see you there then."

"Yeah, you will."

She leaves and I'm swimming in lust, my eyes clouded by a fine red mist of desire.

Joel takes me out to lunch at a Chinese place he knows near the offices, and I sit and eat while he talks about how he got into the industry, slurping down chow mein and trying not to get grease around my mouth.

"I left school, bummed around Europe for a while and just lived off my parents, then I decide I might as well go to university, took a degree in sociology and did another language, Russian. Then while everyone was trying to figure out what graduate opportunities there were, I just hung out in clubs and bars listening to music, speaking to people. A friend was asked by some A&R over at Chrysalis whether he wanted to help him out, get paid for going clubbing and that sort of thing. He knocked him back and sent him on to me, and here I am."

"How did you get from Chrysalis to here?"

"Well Jason was working there as their manager for a few months, got offered the position as director and brought me with him."

"Must think highly of you then?"

"I don't know, I think we just get along together, and I think he wanted at least one friendly face, even though the industry's rather close."

"Inbred."

"Yeah!"

I grab a pork ball and dip it into some sauce, eating it with relish, quickly grabbing another and chucking that down as well.

"So you enjoy being an A&R man then?"

"Yeah, it's really fun, lots of hard work though, late nights and all that, but it's just fun being paid to go clubbing. The demo tapes are hard work."

"Why?"

"Most of 'em are shite, a lot of people just chuck 'em without listening to them, but you've got to wade through them because there might be one diamond just waiting to be unearthed."

"What sort of demos do you get sent?"

"All kinds, in all kinds of states, everything from indie to rap to gospel. Just about everything. Everyone thinks they can make it, and the amount of knock-backs you have to give is criminal. Sometimes groups change their name but send the same demo."

Eat some more then sit back stuffed, my stomach distended. Watching the people walking by. A courier zooms past, weaving in and out of traffic, and I get the urge to be there with him. Slashing in and out. Doing the demon run. Giving the finger to the taxis. Smile at the memory and pat my stomach. If only Greer could see me now. I had to call and tell Peter that I'd be off the circuit for a while, while my knee healed, so he doesn't know when I'll be back. But I know I've always got a job there if I want it. Peter looks after his boys.

"You ready to go?"

"Yeah."

"Okay, I'll just get the check."

I told Jason that I like to get paid by the week, fuck their payroll system, none of this monthly bollocks. Check my watch and whistle as I pick at the last scraps of food left on the plates before the waitress comes round and clears them away. Joel comes back and we leave, stepping out from the shade of the canopy above us. Walking back the short way to the office.

"So do you think you'll stay with it, then?"

"Depends on how I feel. I might, I don't know. I might not be suited for this kind of work."

"Don't worry, once you get into it it's easy."

Upstairs it's pretty quiet and I sit and answer the phones. Inevitably it's for someone else who's not in, and so I take down the number and the name and put it on the large message board at the front of the office so they can check their messages as soon as they get in. Start to pick through the demo tapes that are everywhere in the room and listen to them on that dastardly hi-fi. Most of them are shite indie trash, lots of guitars and heavy thumping of drums. The lyrics lost in the sound that the instruments are making. Fast-forward through most of them, listening to bits and pieces of each song. Shake my head constantly as I move from one tape to another, wondering why they even went to the effort of even putting their pitiful attempts at musicality on tape. Joel's on the other side of the room taking a call when Ronald comes out of his office.

"Ronald, do you have any better hi-fi equipment to play this on? This stuff's really bad."

Ronald says nothing to me, just looks me up and down before heading off down away from me. Wonder what's wrong with him. Obviously got a very big stick shoved up his arse. Shake it off as nothing and continue to pick through the tapes. trying to bring up some enthusiasm for what I'm listening to. But I can't, it's all so pitiful. Stop and take a quick walk down to the toilets, my heavily weighted stomach leaning mightily on my bladder. Push through the door and lean against the side of the cubicle as I relieve myself, trying not to fall over. My face twisted as I lean on my bruised side. I hope the bastards go down before I have to get naked with Inez. *If we get naked*, I suppose I should be saying. But I want her and I don't know how I would handle getting kicked to the kerb with her. I'd most probably turn into one of those *Fatal Attraction* stalker people, leaving disturbing messages and wailing plaintively for her outside her window.

Get back to my desk and decide to give Steve a ring, see whether he's had any news on that record. I've been round to few places and been rebuffed by some fucking anal sales assistants, looking down on me as if I was totally deranged. But I do it all the time just on the off chance. I humble myself, stick my pride in my back pocket and try again and again. Humming the bars of the song and singing as much of the lyrics as I can remember. and all I keep getting is blank stares and an invitation to leave the shop immediately.

"Hello, can I speak to Steve?"

"Speaking."

"Steve, it's Eder. Any news on that record?"

"Yeah, maybe, maybe…"

My heart leaps into my throat and I wait.

"I've been speaking to a few people, and they say you should give this guy a call. He doesn't have a phone, doesn't believe in them, but he lives down your sides, up Herne Hill way."

"Yeah, I'm listening."

"He sells old funk and rare groove, and people say he's got this fucking huge back catalogue of stuff, goes to the states on a regular basis. People say he's the man."

"Okay, give me the details."

Grab a pen and start scribbling like a nutter, writing furiously to catch all the information that Steve is giving.

"Thanks, Steve, you're a lifesaver."

"Yeah, I know."

"Do you know what time he's open?"

"It's not a shop or anything, he sells 'em from his house. But he's away in America and he doesn't come back till next week, Thursday. That's what I was told anyway."

"Fuck!!!"

"Don't worry, it's only a week."

"That's too fucking long."

"You've been waiting ten years, another week isn't going to make that much of a difference."

"Thanks, that makes me feel a whole lot better."

"I got a question…"

"Yeah?"

"This might seem silly, but why don't you just find out who the DJ is and ask him whether he wants to sell it?"

"I thought about that, but there's no way he'd sell after what happened on that night."

"Why not?"

"You don't want to know. Anyway, I tried to find out who he was but the people who organised it said he was a friend of a friend from the states over for a few weeks and he was doing someone a favour."

"Bummer."

"Yep."

"Okay. I'll see you later, okay? Just got some customers in."

"Yeah, later."

Put the phone down feeling extremely depressed. I had it. Well, I almost had it. It was there within my grasp and then it slipped away like mercury. I could hear that song playing on my set. Playing that heavenly music. I feel down and up at the same time, I feel like I should be doing something, anything, rather than sitting here staring at the phone in front of me. I want to get up and shout, or scream. The adrenalin's still coursing through me at the thought of having that record in my grasp. Hobble over to Joel and wait for him to finish his telephone conversation.

"What time's this showcase thing?"

Joel takes a quick look at his watch.

"It should be starting in the next half hour or so, it's over at the marquee. Some girl called Rosanna."

"What does she sing?"

Joel shrugs.

"What time we leaving?"

"Give me ten minutes, I just got to arrange a meeting with a manager."

Leave him to it as I wander back down the offices. Sit down in front of a Mac and look at the screen saver, the earth rotating really fast across the screen. Move the mouse and look and see whether it's got any games on it. Find it does and slip into a heavy bout of Maelstrom, twisting and spinning across the screen, shooting at everything in sight. Reminding me that I haven't been to Las Vegas in a while and I feel the need to play Daytona. But with the knee playing up it'll have to wait. See if I can get Iago and Joel out to play it. I don't even know if Joel's into arcades, but he will be as soon as I'm finished with him. A tap on my shoulder from Joel and I have to leave the game behind. It'll give me something to play when I'm bored in the office, and I might even be able to take out that top score.

The sun's still blazing down as we walk through Soho to get to the Marquee Club, my shades down over my eyes as

Joel chats on. He is a bit of a talker, but I don't mind as I'm too busy watching the honeys and seeing if you can be cool whilst walking with a cane.

"Do you burn, Joel?"

"What!?"

"Do you smoke weed?"

"Yeah, don't have any on me though."

"That's good."

"Why, do you?"

"I'm a black man, Joel, of course I burn."

"Not everyone does, you know?"

"Everyone I know does."

Slip from sunlight into shade as we move into the club, the darkness of the walls and coolness of the interior a shock after the brightness of the sun. Joel steps to the bouncer and we sort out guest lists and what not. Inside I can hear a voice speaking into a microphone as they go through the soundcheck. Walk in and the place is empty except for the thirty or so music people camped around the bar, drinking bottles of American beer. Joel moves over to them as I watch the dry ice start to smoke and the lights dim. Joel's hob-nobbing with the other A&R people as I stand alone in the centre of the floor. A man fat and balding comes out onto stage and introduces the singer, who dutifully comes out. She's small, about 5'1" or 5'2", dressed up in a long gown which trails behind her, and her eyes are covered in this garish pink eye shadow. She pulls the microphone to her and breathes into it before speaking.

"This is 'Sensitivity'."

I'm looking behind her for the band but there is none. The stage behind her is empty and smoke is billowing forth, covering her and then revealing her as it whips away. I can hear fans, so I assume that's what's making the smoke move in that extremely irritating fashion. A beat starts and she starts to sing. I look at her lips and listen hard. The bitch is lip-synching. The song's some wispy nonsense about love and losing it and some other bollocks, as she pretends to scream out the words over a strangely metallic and computerised backing track. But it's just noise, and idiot noise at that. I walk away from her and back to the bar, where all of the industry bods have dismissed her and are talking amongst themselves. Only some guy in the corner is standing there, transfixed as if she is the second coming. Get to the bar and ask for a double Malibu on ice and sip it gently as her voice cuts into my ears.

"Are they all like this?"

"No, this one's one of the worst, I'm afraid."

"So what happens now?"

"We all stand here and listen to her and then leave."

"Who put this on? Don't tell me that someone actually paid money for this?"

"Her manager organised it, the fat guy who came on earlier. Most probably from the money she's made gigging."

"She's been out in clubs with this?"

"Yeah."

Shake my head in disbelief and sip some more of my drink, leaning against the bar as I pull out my spliff case and light one up. Taking a deep drag. Mein Gott that feels good. I drag on it again and feel it moving down my body in a wonderfully exhilarating way. There are no words to describe the feeling of a good spliff. Especially after you haven't had one for a while. I take another pull and let it simmer in my hand as I blow that vapour out into the atmosphere, having lost the young girl up on stage from my consciousness.

Lido Dido

"It's hot once again. Temperatures going into the nineties and the white people are out getting tans. Here's a tune to get you into that summer feeling. A summer song. A hot song. A happy song. A tune to play in your convertible and for you poor people out there that can't afford a convertible, just open your sunroof and pretend."

The phone rings as the song starts. The guitar riff making me shift and stretch, reach for the phone as the beat comes in, then the lyrics, and I'm smiling as I pick up the phone and hold it towards the speaker.

Doing it in the park,
doing it after dark.
Ohhh yeahhh…

Pull the phone over to my mouth.

"Don't you just love that song?"

It's Greer. He's laughing at the other end.

"What do you want?"

"Thought you might be up for a ride?"

"Fuck off, my body's still healing. I've only just stopped using the cane to walk."

"Yeah, well I thought you might be a quick healer?"

"Well you try going over the bonnet of a car at thirty miles an hour and see what that does for you."

"Anyway, I've got the all-time good time."

"What?"

"Can you swim?"

"I hate swimming."

"It's good for you. It'll make you heal quicker."

"I hate getting water in my eye."

"Well how do you wash then?"

"Very carefully."

"Brockwell Lido, outside pool, naked women, 'nuff weed."

"I don't know, I ain't looking my best."

"You don't have to take off your clothes."

Think about it for a second.

"Okay, what time you want to meet?"

"Now, I want to meet right fucking now, so drag your lazy self out of bed and phone Iago. I want to spend the whole fucking day there, just soaking up the rays and watching naked titties passing by my face."

"Okay, let me call Iago and I'll call you back with a time."

"Okay."

Slap the phone down and roll over. Most of the bruising's gone down, so I'm just left with the odd ache and pain, but my skin's still a horrible fucking colour and I'm definitely not taking my shirt off; don't even know if I should wear shorts with this fucking huge strapping on my knee. Turn and sit up, giving my bollocks a little cuddle before calling Iago and seeing if he's up for it. He is, so I call Greer back and tell him to be round mine in the next half an hour. Get up and head for the shower, letting my bollocks settle back into their normal position.

Mum's sifting through the *Observer*, various parts of it spread across the table as I peer into the fridge looking for breakfast.

"Mum, you want something?"

"No, I'm fine."

Grab some bread and some ham and make a few toasted sandwiches, eating them as soon as they pop out of the toaster. Slapping huge dollops of Flora onto the toast and wedging man-sized slices of ham in between.

"What you reading?"

"Article on how the menopause is brought on by hysterectomies."

"Heavy."

"You should read it."

"You know where to leave it."

Mum has this habit of highlighting articles and putting them up on my wall for me to read and digest. It's Mum's way of keeping me educated and intelligent. She believes that I have a brain and that I'm just refusing to use it. I've read every article that she's put up on my wall, not because I have to but because they were all interesting. Mum being a *Guardian* reader, what do you expect?

"What you been doing?"

"Nothing, mothers do nothing."

"Sarcasm doesn't suit you."

"*Au contraire!*"

"Learning French as well?"

"*Oui, monsieur.*"

Mum smiles one of those irritatingly irritating mother smiles whilst I lick my wounds and pull out some juice.

"Why didn't we go to church on Sundays?"

"I don't like church, I've never liked church."

"What's wrong with church?"

"Too many religious types there."

"Went through a bad experience with Granny then?"

"Yep."

"Really, why didn't we go to church?"

"Didn't seem much point. The Old Lady taking me to church didn't make much of an impression on me, so I didn't see much point in taking you."

"So you stopped me from going to church?"

"If you'd wanted to go, you could have gone."

"Yeah, twelve-year-old boy goes to church alone, I can see that."

"If you believe, you believe. I don't have that blind faith. I question too much, as the Old Lady says, Y is a letter with a very long tail."

"That makes no sense whatsoever."

"That's why your grandmother is your grandmother and I'm your mother."

"That makes no sense either. If you'd taken me to church I might be in university now."

"No you wouldn't."

"Why not?"

"You can't do DJ degrees."

"Funny."

"Funny ha ha or funny weird?"

"Funny weird."

"That's what I get for giving birth to a son."

Greer's taller than me; he's taller than most people. But I don't hold it against him really, he's too nice for that. Too intent on looking after people and seeing that they do well for you to hold it against him. He's tall but he carries it well. He doesn't have that hunched-over, "I've had to lower my head to get through doors all my life" look about him. Greer being so tall is the reason he's sitting in the front and I'm the poor nigga who's forced to sit in the back. The thing I've found out about

Minis is that you get into them, into the back, and you think, Shit, there's more space than I thought back here, then the seat slides back and it's like, no, there isn't.

Even though Greer's big, he doesn't feel it. He has no great presence. Whenever he's around, I'm always surprised to have to look up at him, because I always feel that he's the same height as me. I love him like a brother, but he's got to get rid of those bullshit dreads, they just do not drop. Fucking Jekyll if you want my opinion.

I grab hold of the headrests as Iago takes us around corners on two wheels. My shades low over my eyes, blocking the harshest of the sun's rays. Iago's going back to the stack with the tunes in the car today. PE and Big Daddy Kane. We sing along, our voices raised as each of us sings a verse. Memories of nights at the Fridge doing shuffle in my Jordans and wearing my hooded parka come flooding back. Old-skool flow rolls around me and I feel to lean back, but there's no room, so I stay where I am.

As usual the volume in the car is ear-shatteringly loud. I don't know how he stands it day in and day out. Since Iago doesn't ride, he drives everywhere. We have a pact: no tubes, no buses. Bad memories from school, it's too easy to get ambushed on public transport. He travels everywhere in his car with the volume whacked up. Imagine standing in a club beside the speaker every time you drive. That's what it's like in Iago's car. Sound so loud and clear that you should not even contemplate stepping near the car with even the slightest hangover. If you're not used to it, it'll grate on you. No, not grate, rasp along your nerves with no end in sight.

A quick left, a quick right. Then down a tree-lined street. Iago's peering off into the distance when Greer's arm whips out pointing off to the right. Iago's head snaps up, doesn't check his mirrors and we're hand-braked into a slide. The back end snaps around and white tyre smoke is pouring around the car. The stink of burning rubber is as thick as the smoke. The music isn't an issue anymore. It's the noise of an engine roaring, tyres squealing and Greer's throat being screamed red raw as he experiences the full intensity of a drive with Iago. The world stops moving and we're parked in front of the steps leading up to Brockwell Lido, hard up against the kerb. Look behind me and see the trail of skid marks telling the story of how we got here. Greer's as white as I've ever seen him, and I hear him wheezing and I'm afraid that he might be hyperventilating.

Iago's already out and I've got to give Greer a big push to get him out of the door. Iago stops as he gets to the steps and looks back, waving at us to come on. When he gets out, Greer can hardly stand and I have to let him lean on the car for a few seconds.

"Does he always drive like that?"

"Yep. Just be glad you're not with him when he hits the motorways."

Greer looks at me shocked and walks slowly up the steps after Iago.

"Come on, what are you two waiting for?"

"Since you almost killed me, I feel walking a little slowly is justified."

"You wouldn't have died!"

"What do you know, you weren't the one sitting in the passenger seat with his life flashing before his eyes."

"Handbrake turns aren't dangerous, and I was only doing fifty. No cars on the road, plenty of space to slide into, what were you worried about?"

"My life, my life!"

I'm keeping well out of it as we walk up to the ticket booth and hand over our shekels. Greer forgets the conversation as his eyes lock onto the chest of some girl. She's wearing a white shirt over her bikini and a brightly coloured wrap-around skirt. Look at her face and decide she's not all that, swivel my head and find there are more like her all around. Towels clutched in painted nails, bikinis already on and hair tied back.

From inside I can hear screaming children and splashing water. People having fun, a sound you rarely hear between October and March. The deep depressive quality of winter blanketing everything. Faintly, behind all the sounds of merriment, I can hear music, some Jodeci. The sun's out and people are enjoying it. The women are half naked and drugs are freely available. Move through the turnstiles, from the semi-darkness and shade into the scorching sunlight that pours across the body.

Poolside is ram with people even this early. Children running along the side of the pool before diving in, one foot raised and a scream escaping their throats. Mothers watch from towels on the other side of the pool, while middle-aged men, pasty white with guts, pour over the Sunday supplement. The floor is awash with people lying on their towels, eyes closed and the sun-tan lotion heavily applied. Bare flesh glistening under the yellow light. Faces are turned to the sun, as are backs and breasts. Leaning on straightened arms with necks stretched to the limit. The most pressing desire of everyone over sixteen is to get a tan. The deepest, darkest all-over-body tan possible.

Iago gives me a tug on my arm to get me moving with the collective as I stand staring at all the bare flesh. There is just so much of it. So much skin, it's like flicking through a porno mag. I watch where I step as we ease our way round to the other side of the pool and look for a place to sit and relax. A secluded corner to puff away, not that anyone's on the lookout for druggies. People are lying everywhere, towels thrown across the floor marking territory. Greer's already staked his claim and is waving at us to make our way over there before shit gets taken. He's claimed his spot by a series of long steps which is just a heaving mass of flesh. Spread our towels and sit for a second, just soaking up the atmosphere.

"What do you think?"

"Nice."

"Don't you ever say anything other than nice?"

"Okay, it's fucking class."

"That's better."

Greer pulls off his top and chucks it onto his towel. Stands up and does an impressive series of upper-body warming-up techniques.

"You coming in?"

"No, I'm never coming in."

"You will."

He leaves me thinking what the fuck is he talking about, 'cause he ain't getting me to swim in that chlorine saturated muck, as he eases through the crowd to get to the pool. Standing at its edge before cutting cleanly into the water and starting to swim laps. Around him people are moving through the water, some splashing and playing, others doing some serious swimming. Kids going tanking over the edge in various contortions. Youthful limbs flailing before they crash into the foaming water. Each splash echoing around the open-air arena. I could never understand why anyone would want to drown on purpose and get that stinging in their eyes.

I pull out a spliff as I watch and light it up. Iago's pulled out a hi-fi mag and is reading it as he lies half naked beneath the sun. People are either sunbathing or conversing, their conversations filtering into the cacophony of sound that is all around. Just another layer on the aural onion. Watch the sunglasses catching the light and hiding people's eyes. Look at the names on them, Ray-Ban, Diesel, Police. Some fucking bod wearing my Oakleys. God, I hate those bastards that wear Oakleys and have never been anywhere near a bike since they used to play on their tricycles. Wearing their E-Wires, or Frog Skins, M-Wires, or Sub-Zeros. It just fucking pisses me off. Is nothing safe from fashion's gaze? I only wear my Oakleys when I ride. You need them, otherwise my eyes would be a second home to flies and grit. I use them for a reason, they have a function which they perform well. I don't wear them for the fashion credibility that it gives me. Fashion is fly-by-night, but function is eternal.

My eyes sweep the poolside area, watching, ever watching, as the women sun themselves. Pulling my glasses low onto my nose so that I can peer over them and let them know that I am watching. So many different shapes and sizes and ages. I try not to be obvious as I stare at their breasts, but I can't help it. They are all just so luscious and ripe. Nipples outstanding and the roundness of them so appealing. Pert breast, pendulous breasts, medium-sized breast, small breasts, breasts with large nipples, breasts with long nipples, breasts that are offset, breasts that are very regular, spread out or close together. So many breast that you forget to look at the faces above them, my eyes are just locked onto their chests. The chest is all important, because that is what is being displayed. So I watch the display, trying to differentiate between them.

Take another toke on the joint and feel it turn me into molten butter. Toke long on it. Haze surrounds me. Look into a girl's eyes as her head turns and her gaze slides past me. Naked people are so vulnerable, so pale and soft. Looking at them I shiver and feel my own vulnerability. All that flesh so easily scarred and disfigured. Bruised and battered. My arm rubs my injured side as I think about it. Tracing the edges of the bruising, mapping out its area and its texture. My fingertips sliding underneath my T-shirt to fully feel it. Feel the texture change and the hardening of my skin, the flakiness of it as it starts to peel away. Stop myself from hauling on the scabs that have appeared. If I see a scab, I instantly want to peel it away, getting rid of that hardened skin.

Look at the flesh around me, all of it wrinkled, smooth, freckled and spotty. Oiled, wet and shiny. The odd hairy mole and the bright-red-lobster colouration that some are carrying in. Take another toke and hold the smoke deep, puff out my cheeks like Dizzy before exhaling. Scratch my nose and look at the spliff between my fingers. Contemplation like this is not good for me. Too much thought shrinks the brain, causes a slowing of reaction. Try and think while you ride and you get fucked.

Hand the J over to Iago before searching in my pocket and coming out with the address Steve gave me. Look at the writing on it. My own and the address. Smooth out the creased slip and just stare at it. Making the decision to go and visit it once we finish here. I know where it is because I've been round there every night since I got the address from Steve, keeping my own vigil outside the empty house. Hoping each night that the lights will be on and that I can go inside and see whether my search is over. The song repeating over and over in my head, the lyrics swirling around on the tip of my tongue. I know if I ever hear it again I'll be able to sing it all, without a missed word or a fumble. So deeply embedded in me is it.

Shake my head and fold the paper back up carefully before putting it back into my pocket.

A bikinied butt shimmies past and "I want some dark brown sugar" slips from my lips as my eyes covet what is passing. The urge to stretch out my hand and run my fingertips across the curve of her flank is unbearable. I resist and let her walk on unmolested. She moves slowly past, trying not to step on anything or anyone. A short mincing step, as if she's wearing high heels. But her foot's bare, the toes red, thick with polish and her foot bottom black like the ace of spades. She must be one of those idiots that decide to cast away shoes when the sun comes out and walk the streets barefoot. Just looking at it all dark and dusty causes my eyes to close and a shiver to run through me. All attraction disappears, head turns and she is dismissed.

A man must always look at a woman's footwear, it shows what type of woman she be. If her footwear be dodgy, don't even think about stepping to it. Footwear to avoid includes sandals, those dodgy new-age bastards; not even those newfangled Nike and Reebok varieties can redeem them. Loafers. Aarrgh. Fucking Sloane, too much money and not enough sense. And if they're not a Sloane they're a tourist, some foreign country where they are fashionable. Dodgy trainers, usually Vans, Airwalk or Converse, beloved by the fashion victim brigade, too interested in how they look. Also those dodgy — well fucking dodgy — platform trainers from Chevignon. Avoid, avoid. And last but not least, Doctor Martens, the high ones, in a various multitude of colours, staple footwear of the grunge woman, the indie kid. There is no redemption for this type of footwear.

A shadow passes over me and stops. Look up and Greer's

back from his swimming exploits, dripping over me. Grabs his towel and starts to dry himself vigorously.

"You should come in, water's lovely."

"Nah, I'll just enjoy the view."

"How are going to enjoy yourself if you don't take off your shirt? You can't even get a tan."

"You haven't seen the amount of bruises I've got."

"That's right, you haven't shown me your scars of battle yet."

"Too disgusting for your weak heart."

"Really?"

"Really."

He finishes drying off and Iago hands him the roach-end of the joint we've been enjoying.

"Okay, promise you won't faint?"

"Promise."

Feeling very self-conscious, I peel off my T-shirt, showing to the whole world my bruised and battered body. Greer's low whistle is enough to confirm what I already knew: that my body looks disgusting.

"Nasty."

"It looked worse."

I can see what they are looking at the large mass of yellow bruising along my shoulder and side. A long scar of scabby flesh, right at the point where I hit the ground and the skin was scrapped off. I didn't realise I was bleeding until the ambulance took me to hospital. The bruising extending from my shoulder down to and around my abdomen. Look around to see whether anyone else is watching; no one is, but it doesn't make me feel any better. I can still feel eyes on me. People watching and drawing in breath at the extent of the disfigurement. After giving Greer and Iago a good long chance to look at it, I pull on my T-shirt and feel much more confident straight away.

"What you put your shirt back on for?"

"I don't like people to see my scars, private property."

"Why? Everyone's seen scars before."

"Not mine they haven't."

Greer shakes his head and sits down in front of us.

"How's the job going?"

"What job?"

"The guy that took me out gave me a job at the record label that he works for."

"You sneaky bastard. Have you told Peter yet?"

"No, I'm going to give it a few weeks and see how it turns out first."

"What are you doing?"

"I'm an A&R scout, searching for new talent, the next Take That."

"Really?"

"Yeah."

"What label you working for?"

"Zefal."

"Big company."

"Yep, got a lot of people on their books."

"So what else do you do apart from snort coke? I hear everyone in the industry does it."

"I answer phones, listen to demo tapes. All of them are shite, I could do better myself."

"Why don't you?"

"Listen, I'm talking here, don't interrupt."

"Go on then."

"Where was I. Oh yeah, listen to demos, most of them are crap, go to showcases of artists, most of those are crap as well.

Those happen in the afternoon, then you go out clubbing in the evening. Some of the people I work with go to pubs and listen to live bands and stuff. I don't really know what I'm doing yet. They don't seem to have any interest in black music unless it's coming from the States. It's difficult."

"So you're getting paid to go clubbing."

"Basically."

"Shit, I could do that."

"I know."

"So you going to keep at it?"

"I don't know, it's good money, but I feel useless. I don't know enough people, industry people. So that I can get some feedback about who's good and who's shit. Right now I'm just flying solo."

"Sign some jungle acts, man."

"Jungle's too black for them, they don't understand it. You should see it, I'm the only fucking black face there. Fucking scary. I've been speaking to a few people and it all comes down to money. The whole thing runs on greed, if it ain't making money it gets kicked to the kerb."

"Sign some jungle."

"What is with you? I don't know how yet. I don't know what strings to pull or what buttons to push. I was speaking to this guy over at Sony and he was telling me if you want to get anything out, you've got to fight for it, and even then, the marketing bastards'll cut your throat because even though you've got the tune cut and mixed, you've still got to get it out there, and they won't stump up the cash for videos or posters or anything unless they know it's going to come back with some cash for them."

"Shit."

"Exactly. Jungle won't get off the ground because to get it

mainstream you have to dilute it so ordinary white blokes in the street can understand it. So you, me and every other nigga says sellout and it goes underground again. The marketing men just want acts that sell a million copies and gets onto *Top of the Pops*. And the music that I want ain't going that way. Imagine Old 'Dirtee on *Top of the Pops*. It don't gel.

"I know what you're saying. White people don't want to know about black culture, but we have to understand white culture because we're living in it and we're part of it. The only white people that are a part of black culture are the ones that have been brought up on council estates and been to the same schools and lived the same life."

"I hear ya."

Pull out another spliff and spark it, feel like pushing my lighter in the air.

Original bad bwoy dem is in here...

I love the feel of summer, the scent of summer, the look of summer. The brightness of it, when everything is glowing and bright. Even the brown grass, dried out by the sun and worn smooth by the passing of feet over it, is bright. Every day is like carnival, every moment is precious and glorious, carefree and exuberant. I can't wait for tomorrow to arrive, for the sun to rise again. Moving from sunshine to shade, heat to coolness. Wandering in search of a cooling breeze, a breath of wind. It amazes me how many people seem to inhabit London during the summer. The city becomes filled with people, bursting at the seams as they just appear out of nowhere. Everyone wearing practically nothing, and it doesn't matter what shape your body is. How fat or thin. Everyone showing what they got, because for an all-too-brief moment, the sun is out.

Summer is all about exposure, sexual heat. All the man that train during the winter, loading up their bodies with excess muscle. They do it for this time, when they can rip their clothes off, hulk-like, and expose the rippling flesh beneath. The definition, the cut. Their unbridled strength. Even though they look like balloons and the smallest prick would cause them to deflate. The friction that they generate from their flesh rubbing together putting at least a degree on the overall temperature. Preening and posturing, their bodies ,shouting, "Look at me, look at me, aren't I attractive."

Summer is the season of flirting, of eye contact, shy smiles and bold glances. Of desiring and wanting someone. Short skirts and bare flesh. Stomachs gaining sunlight and jackets wrapped tight around childbearing hips. Hips that move and sway intoxicatingly as they walk. Trees dancing in the breeze, performing a flamenco. All passion and expression. I could watch them all day long, matching my moods to theirs. During summer they dance and sway and I want to dance with them, place my body in rhythm with them. Lean on them and feel their movement through the bark.

Hand the spliff over to Iago and get up, stretching my legs.

"Do you want anything?"

"Nah, I'm fine."

Look at Greer, who shakes his head. Move through the people sitting or lying and step carefully over them, making my way to the little clubhouse where I can buy a drink. Stand behind two children shouting about who can dive the furthest, recounting what they've done only minutes before. My eyes constantly moving over the people out at the lido. Out in the sunshine. Look over the shoulder of a woman in front of me, and stare down into her cleavage, see the pools of water rolling across her breasts. Order my drink and wait while it arrives, popping it open and sipping from it as I make my way back.

Put my body back into my little space and sit with my hands on my knees sipping every so often from my drink.

The House

We pull up outside it and I feel a thrill run through me. One of the lights is on, down in the front. I'm urging Greer to get out as I pop out, pain in my knee forgotten as I run towards the house. Ringing the bell like crazy. Breath coming fast and my heart up in my throat. It takes an age for the light to come on in the hall and I can see a form through the glass door walking towards me. It opens and a man in his early fifties stands in front of me, a dark beard sprinkled with white covering his lower face. A large mop of unruly hair like Don King's on his head. He's in a T-shirt, stretched to cover the gut hanging over his belt, khaki shorts, hairy legs tree trunk–like beneath. On his feet are a pair of old Jesus creepers, his socks peeping through the open toe.

"Hi, are you Graham?"

"Yes."

"My friend got me your address. I'm looking for this record that I haven't heard in ages, and he told me you might have it."

"He did, did he?"

"Yeah, and I was wondering whether you might know it. And if you did have it whether you would sell it to me."

He looks me up and down and I stand there expectantly. Hope filling me up as I wait.

"You'd better come in then."

I follow him down the hall, waving a hand at Iago to stay in the car. He opens the door to his sitting room and I enter into vinyl paradise.

Everywhere I look is vinyl, long rows of it on homemade shelves. There's no room for chairs because everywhere is vinyl. Every corner is submerged beneath vinyl. I take a deep breath as I look at the rows upon rows of vinyl and feel my prayers have been answered. Graham walks deeper into his vinyl cavern and I see that actually there are two chairs deep behind a pile of records. He sits and offers me a chair, which I gladly accept. Looking around, eyes wide in wonder.

"This is some collection you've got."

"There's more upstairs. I just keep the ones that I play down here."

"You play all of these?"

"I don't buy them to look at them."

"I'm sorry, it's just you've got so much. I haven't got half as much as this and I can't find time to play all of those."

"You make time, you make time."

We sit in silence for a while before I shake myself into speaking again.

"Well the song I want goes like this…"

I clear my throat and start to hum the first few bars, then the beat, but I keep stopping as I'm so nervous. Calm myself and manage to hum the beat without stumbling before launching into a quavering rendition of the first few lines of the song, about as much as I can remember of the lyrics. Graham's staring at me intently as I'm going through all of this, his gaze never wavering. I stop and he's still staring at me.

"What do you think?"

"I know it."

My heart leaps and I feel as if I'm going to die. At last, at last.

"Do you have it? What's it called?"

Questions rolling one into the other as I try to gather as much information as possible.

"I don't have it. It's really rather rare."

"Do you know someone who does?"

"No one that I know has a copy. As far as I know, they never pressed it up fully, just a few acetates floated round that no one ever had the guts to play."

I can feel myself falling deeper and deeper into a pit of bitter despair. Tears move to the backs of my eyes and I can feel my throat tightening as they threaten to fall. I can hardly get the words out.

"But I heard a DJ playing it a few weeks back."

"I don't know how he got one, lucky bastard. Maybe he knows people in America. As far as I know, they maybe — and I stress the 'maybe' — pressed up five, maybe six copies, and those are all in America, none ever got over here."

I can't speak, I just lower my head and try to hold back the tears.

"I've been searching for it for ages. Ages."

I can't even look at him. Don't want to believe that there is no light at the end of the tunnel. No happy ending, no joyous reunion.

"Shit."

"It's called 'One last time,' it's by Julianne Wilson and Fred Wesley."

I sit there for a long time, fighting back the tears, before I get up and walk out of that marvellous room, down the corridor and out into the humid night. Stand on the steps as I hear the door close behind me like one of those doors in horror movies, with a loud boom and thud. Breathe deep as my chest threatens to tighten up on me. Clamping tight and making it difficult to draw breath. I don't want to sit in the car. I don't want to explain what happened. I don't want to talk about it. I want to just sit on these steps and cry. Salty tears are trailing their way down my cheeks. I sniff and clear my throat before making that dreaded walk back to my friends and the inevitable questions.

Shit Happens

Cool. Calm. Unremitting darkness consumes me. I'm caught. No way out. No amount of record playing can pull me out of this blue funk that I've slipped into. Shadows surround me. Smoke billows from my mouth. A cloud of desolation. Trapped here and no way to leave. Event horizon spiralling down into an abyss. A realm of dislocation, once entered, never left. Sucking me in. My actions hold no meaning and as I sit, I smoke, quiet and contained, encased in inky surrounds.

The deep red glow of my cigarette fractured and pitted. Molten lava head suspended in space. The only indication that I am still alive. Still here, not just a vacant shell, an empty vessel. Not speaking, not thinking, just breathing out smoke. A smoke dragon appearing from nowhere, impacting with the force of nature, ripping through all that is thought and known. Tornado fierce, whirlwind harsh. Silent destruction appearing, revealing, disappearing.

As I sit, I think that my life is irredeemable, caught within a vortex over which I have no control. Given hope only for it to be torn away. I smoke, dragging that nicotine-infected smoke inside of me. I don't even like cigarettes. Smoke wreathes me, gliding around me like flying serpents. Hissing as their number is increased. Crimson-glowing tip exuding a hypnotic force. I stare dumbly at it, feeling bereft. That which I searched for is gone. I will never find it and it has left a gaping hole in me. I tell myself that it was only a record. Just a piece of vinyl. A thing, an object. Not a human being. But no matter the words

I use to try and convince myself they have no affect. I still sit here in this smoke-filled mausoleum.

Around me my records lie silent. They have no power to move me anymore, no power to kindle any feelings or emotions. My whole being was caught up in that one piece of vinyl, that twelve inches of round existence. Not with a bang but with a whimper. I berate myself for not trying harder, for not searching harder. How can this crushing weight that sits on me have been brought about by this one record. Just one record. Even though I searched for it, I torment myself with the thought that if I had tried harder, gone that extra mile, it would be in my possession right at this minute. It would be playing, coming through my speakers, clearly and precisely.

My life feels like a tomb of memories, decrepit, decaying and visited only fitfully when the pain of not looking is greater than the pain of looking. I have disappeared into a vortex of deadened sensation. Nothing can hurt me as much as I hurt myself over the loss of this record. One last time. The title is anathema to me. To even think the words much less say them is like acid on my tongue. Yet repeatedly my tongue is burnt as the words fall upon them.

I need to sleep.

Stub out the cigarette I've just lit. The humid night whispering that I won't get to sleep, that this non-life I am living will not change and only in my darkest fog-bound, Morpheus-encased delirium visitations will I find peace. Only when the intro, eerily ethereal, swirls around me will I find peace, only to wake and despair for I do not have it.

I desire sleep, but I force myself to go to my decks. Fire them up and turn down my amp. Pull it back, not thinking about what I am doing, just going through the motions. Everything goes through the motions. Just a pawn under the command of some omnipresent Machiavelli.

The streetlamps cast long shadows and the trees stand as if dead. Long-dead kings, silent and imposing. No movement, mourning the passing of their time.

Drop the needle in and let the beat come to me. I'm always surprised by the way sound expands at night. No matter how quiet I turn it down, it still seems loud. Bass envelops me.

If you look at my life
and see what I've seen...

I whisper the words so quietly that my voice grows hoarse and rough. Dry, no lubrication, as I try and sing in key with Mary J.

Tears start to roll, soft and secretive. I cry for her, for that record that should have been mine.

...see what I've seen...

Quiet and introspective, my desire lost.

Out of Control

I sit in the office depressed. Not even the sun's rays flooding over me can lift my depression. Everyone in the office looked at me strangely when I came through the door, but I didn't care. I didn't give a fuck. The depression had me tight and nothing was pulling me away from it. Not even the new system that sits beside my desk. A NAD amp, Thorens deck, Nakamichi tape deck and some CD player, all hooked by to a nice pair of warm bassy Wharfedales. I couldn't even be bothered to play with it. To touch it let alone look at it. Turn my chair away and sit staring at the blank piece of paper in front of me.

Ronald comes out of his office and looks towards me. He don't like me, but fuck him. He hasn't just lost something that he's been searching for for ten years, has he? No, he's just sitting in his office bitching about some fuckwit who doesn't know the first thing about the industry phoning him up and asking silly questions about how he can get his band signed.

I shouldn't have come in, but I couldn't bear to stay in my room another day, and I'd already taken two days off work. I might not like this job too fucking much, but at the moment it's the only one I've got. I move my legs under the table and shift their position from here to there. Not that it makes a great deal of difference. The heaviness in my heart still refuses to shift.

The only other time I've felt this bad was when I split with Eve, and that lasted a good few months. Every woman I saw who looked like her would become her, and my heart would leap and I'd think, Yes, this is it, I'll see her again, speak to her again. But it wasn't her. It's been two years now since we split. I had visions of marriage, children, lifelong commitment. They all hit the fan when she said she was going to live in New Zealand with her parents.

Pull myself up from the table and go to the drinks machine down the hall. Search for some change and pull out a fifty-pence piece. Exact change only. Step to the other side and ask Janice for some change. She gives it to me, looking at me as if I've become a wino or something. Take it and put it into the machine, press the button for a Coke and wait. Nothing happens. No thumping sound, no internal noise. The red light isn't on, so there are cans in there. Press another button for a Lilt. Nothing doing. Press all the buttons one at a time, one after the other, with a mounting feeling that the whole fucking world is against me. Nothing doing. Grab hold of the machine and tug it, pulling on it, rocking it back and forth. Fucker. My teeth gritting as I rock.

"Give me my drink."

Let go of it and kick it, step back and slam my foot into it. Step back again and kick it. Feeling my leg jar all the way to my hip. I'm using my good foot and perching precariously on my bad one. Give it another good kick, but nothing happens. Lean forward panting and slam my forehead against it until I start to feel dizzy. Turn and slide down it to the floor, and as I descend see that the whole floor is looking at me and I don't care. My whole life has turned to shit and this fucking drinks machine has swallowed up my money. Put my head in my hands and close my eyes.

"You feeling alright?"

"Leave me the fuck alone."

I don't know who it is and I don't care, I just want them to get their hand off my shoulder and leave me be. Pull myself off the floor and head to the toilets, ignoring the stares of those around me. Fuck 'em, fuck 'em all. Step into the toilet and open the windows before going into the cubicle nearest them and locking the door. Put down the seat and sit there, contemplating the spliff that I hold in my hand. To light or not to light, that is the question. Who am I kidding?

Spark it and puff deep and I don't stop puffing till I'm pulling on roach and my lids feel heavy. I only put a little bit of tobacco in it, wrapping it around a large section of weed, and a little bit of solid that I found at the bottom of my bag. I sit in the toilet, my head low, listening to the people moving around outside, wondering when the next man's going to decide to come and use the toilet. All power to him if he can fight his way through the smoke.

Try not to think about the record, but it is just there at the forefront of my mind all the time. Even the amount of weed that I've consumed can't make it go away. I feel I need to get out of London, go somewhere, maybe Amsterdam, and get smashed on a regular basis. Try different types of weed and experience different sensations from it. Maybe I need a holiday, I haven't been out of the country in ages, not since Mum's last trip to Italy a few years back, straight after I split with Eve.

Pull out another spliff and spark it up, trying mightily to just take the edge off the depression curling around me. Feeling like death warmed up. I sit here and wonder what the fuck am I doing. Suddenly I don't feel like finishing the spliff. Stub it out and open up the cubicle. Step out and stand in front of the long mirror above the row of sinks. Stare at myself in the mirror, breaking down my face into its constituent parts. Eyes, nose, lips, ears, cheekbones, forehead, chin. Look at it with a critical eye, see the redness of my eyes, if anyone looks at me I've either been crying or puffing. Lean my head against the glass and tap it gently with my forehead.

I walk back down to my desk and I can feel the eyes on me and I know they're watching me. It isn't my paranoia overtaking me. Feel them assessing me, wondering what is wrong with me, why I am taking myself to the wall, over what. Has he broken up with his girlfriend? Someone died? Learned he's got an illness? What? What?

I'm not going to tell them, they'd laugh at me, make a joke over something that is precious to me. I stand at my desk and then slowly sink into my chair, feeling the cushioning of it supporting me. The phone rings and I let it, let someone else get it, I'm tired. Put my head on my arms and close my eyes.

I'm woken by a rough shoving on my arm. Joel leaning over me.

"Leave me alone."

"What's the matter?"

"Nothing's the matter."

"So what are you acting like this for?"

"I'm on my period."

Joel gives me a sharp look.

"If they can get away with it, why can't I?"

"Snap out of it."

"That is probably the most stupid thing you've ever said in your life, ever."

Look down at my watch. Half four. Can't believe I've been asleep for over three hours.

"Do I snore?"

"What?"

"Do I snore?"

"No."

"Good."

Push away from the desk, lean backwards and stretch out the sleep from me. I still feel like shit, but sometimes you've got to go through the motions.

"Come on."

"Where we going?"

"Going to a studio to have a look at an act recording their first single."

"Not going."

"Get up."

Let him haul me to my feet and drag me out of the office and onto the street, offering little resistance as we bundle into a cab and lurch into rush-hour traffic.

"Who we going to see?"

"Who do you think?"

"What, Innuendo?"

"Give a prize to the man in the grouchy hat."

"Haven't they recorded anything yet?"

"Just a demo on a 4-track set. Now were seeing what they sound like with the works behind them."

Sit in silence the rest of the way as the cab weaves its way through the centre of London, forcing a path for itself through the reluctant commuters. Think to myself that it might be on a compilation somewhere, that there is still hope. Only to slap it down with the thought that if it wasn't released properly, how would enough people have heard about it for it to get on a compilation? It's most probably lying gathering dust in a barn in the Deep South somewhere.

The blue funk contains me within a quiet solitary shell. It

holds me there and I do not want to break free of it. I do not want to make myself whole, the effort feels too large. So I sit and condemn myself for being a fool and try to snap out of it, but know that I am incapable.

The taxi pulls up near Swiss Cottage and we hop out. Joel all energy and life as I trudge behind him to a converted church, with a sign outside saying Trinity Studios. Lean on the intercom and wait for the huge double doors to swing open. A voice comes back allowing us entry and Joel pushes. The doors swing as if they are feather light and we enter into the inner sanctum. In front of us is a reception area, with gold and platinum records strung along the walls. To our immediate left is a kitchen area with a few studio people making each other coffee and toast. But rising up behind the reception area is a split-level interior, which only as we make our way up the spiral staircase do we see is split like this all the way to the back. Walk along a balcony, alongside which there are doors with little glass windows through which you can peep in and see the back of some engineer or producer leaning over a mixing desk, and further back still through the glass panel separating them, the artist singing their heart out. I peek into every door to see whether I can see someone famous before Joel pulls open the door to studio 7B.

We step in and Joel introduces me to the engineer and the producer, who sit conversing at the desk. Look around the studio and see the large monitor speakers mounted on the wall, the large sofa set behind the desk and the small fridge beside it. On the table in front of the sofa is a bowl of fresh fruit and some magazines. Through the glass panels, the girls are standing beside hanging microphones with those mesh covers in front of them. Headphones held tightly to their ears. They are conferring between themselves as they wait for their next take on the song they are recording. I sit in the sofa and their manager, a rather large woman dressed in what looks like a duvet cover, swans into the room, her voice deep and disconcerting. Her chins wobble as she talks at Joel,

"Oh, Joel darling, the girls aren't happy with their accommodation, you've got to sort that out. Oh, and also they need a new vocal coach. Their old one was a bit of a bitch, so we got rid of her, and they haven't got a thing to wear, we're getting severe press coverage and the girls need to look good. Got all of that, Joel? Good, ta-ta. Phone calls to make, meetings to arrange."

Then she swans out again, duvet swishing behind her.

"If she were talking to me like that I would have kicked her to the kerb."

"I know, but you got to do it. You got to make sure everyone's happy. I suppose I should be grateful at least the band and the manager are still talking to each other."

"That's not the point, you're not her lackey."

"But I am, I have to make sure everything runs smoothly. I have to drop everything and make sure everyone's needs are met, because if they're not, then everything falls apart and we have no product."

"Cutthroat."

"No, I love it."

"I was talking about the industry."

Sit for a while eating banana's, chucking the skins into the bin over in the corner. But just sitting here makes me feel uncomfortable. What am I doing in here? Absolutely nothing, I give Joel a wave as I duck out the room, saying I'm going to the toilet, before asking the receptionist if I could use her phone. Ring Iago at work, look at my watch, hope he hasn't left yet. I'm glad when he answers.

"Yeah?"

"Can you come and pick me up, I'm at Swiss Cottage, Trinity Studios."

"Yeah, I'll be there as fast as I can. You feeling better?"

"No."

"You will do."

He puts down the phone enigmatically and I sit outside on the steps watching the sun slowly move across the sky, getting closer and closer to the horizon. Pull out a spliff and toke on it as commuters rush past heading for the tube. Each one wrapped up in their own little nine-to-five universe. Watch them look down at their shoes and wonder what's so interesting about the concrete in front of them. Not wanting to be aware of the world around you is a crime. But who am I kidding, I've locked myself out of everyone's lives for the past few days, sitting in my room and puffing like a demon to keep the pain away. See the furtive stares I'm given as the commuters see what I'm smoking. Just smile condescendingly at them and they hurry on. Twist the spliff between my fingers and watch the end glow then start to blacken as it goes out, before bringing it back to my lips and pulling it back to life.

I check my watch for the sixth time as Iago hauls up in front of the studios, leaning across and popping open the passenger door. Walk down the steps and slide into the car. For a change he hasn't got the music whacked up to the edge of insensibility. Just soft and lilting. He pulls away from the kerb in a hurry.

"Where we going?"

"Wait and see."

We drive in silence, me handing the spliff over to him,

Iago doing the "spliffs stick to my bottom lip" trick. From the speakers, Curtis sings "Pusherman".

I'm your momma,
I'm your daddy...

Nod my head and close my eyes, sink into the seat and for a short period of time sleep a dreamless sleep. No images of the record slanting across my lids. Tortured images of me chasing the record and it forever beyond my reach. None of that, just plain old-fashioned darkness. The huskiness of Curtis's voice sending me away, like a small boat over a big loch.

I'm woken by Iago dragging me out of the car, his record bag slung over his shoulder and heavy by the looks of it. He pulls me out and I look up. We're in front of Dean's tower block, wonder what we're doing here.

"Come on."

He drags me forth before I shake off his hand and walk along unassisted beside him.

"What're we doing?"

"You're pitiful."

"What?"

"You heard me. How can you act this fucking cut up over a record? You weren't this bad when Danny died."

"I loved Danny, he was my friend."

"Yeah, but I didn't see you lock yourself in your room for four days and torture everyone around you. You carried on, you cried, you hurt, but it didn't swamp you like this. And this is over what, a record?"

"Not just a record, *the* record. If I hadn't heard it, I wouldn't be me, I wouldn't be here. Do you understand? That record made me what I am."

"Bullshit, no record has that much of an effect on a person. No record."

"We'll just have to agree to disagree."

"Not if we're going to continue to be friends, we're not."

"What?"

"I don't want no fucking solitary nigga saying his life ain't worth living 'cause he ain't got a record. Fuck that. If you want to keep that up, you can find another friend to carry you."

We travel up in the lift and I stare at him, at this man who is my friend, and the feeling that I might lose him as I lost Danny terrifies me. Friends are precious, all the moreso because their friendship can be taken away at any time. You are not bound by bonds of blood and familial duty. I can't say anything so I turn my head away and watch the lights light up as we travel upwards: 19. 20. 21. 22. 23. 24.

A bell rings and the doors slide apart. We walk down the dimly lit corridor and lean on the bell. Dean opens up and ushers us in, giving us both quick hugs before we move down to his inner sanctum.

"Do you want something to drink and shit?"

"Nah, we're fine."

Iago speaks for both of us as we follow Dean into his room. The windows letting in the fading light, though it is still bright. Beneath the window are Deans decks, beneath that he has his keyboard and his sampler. To the left of those on a little side table is his Mac, on which he runs his Cubase.

I've always loved drum and bass. I was never interested in the lead singer or the lead guitarist as most white people seem to be. It was always for me the rhythm section, drum and bass, that captivated my attention. I even tried to learn to play. My fingers itching to play those throbbing bass chords, wanting to pluck on the strings as my head snapped back and forth, but even Mr Maguire with his magic hands couldn't get anything resembling a tune from these fingers. Like most DJs, I'm a failed musician. I found I had a knack for making music by mixing other people's records together, and that was where my destiny lay.

Dean's got some big-ass monitors on the floor and his record collection is piled high on the other side of his room, next to his bed. Next to the Mac he's got a little 12-track set up, hooked up to everything, and a Dat machine and an ordinary tape deck to make recordings. Looking on all the lights and plugs, I get the feeling that Dean must have the living electrical bill.

"So what do you guys want to do?"

"We've come to make a jungle track."

"Yeah, I'm up for that."

"Do you have a plan or do you just want to mess around and see what happens?"

"We'll just mess around. You know we've never done it before, so we'll be relying on you a lot."

"Yeah, no sweat. You got your samples."

"Yep."

Iago starts pulling records out of his bag and laying them in a pile beside him.

"Okay, let's go to work."

Dean pulls out a spliff and lights it up as Iago pulls out his first record and lays it on the decks.

"I want the bassline off this one."

He takes a track that should be played at 45 and slows it to 33 so an eerie thumping comes out. Dean nods and bends his head, his face clouded by smoke, and starts to press buttons on the sampler as Iago tweaks the record, spinning it with his finger and changing the pitch slightly, making it go faster and faster before wheeling it and starting it again. Dean nods his head to it and starts the sampler. Iago stops the record and Dean leans over, pressing the keyboard and letting the sample play every time his finger hits a key.

"You got some disks?"

"Nah."

"Don't worry, I got some spare."

Dean turns and bends backwards, pulling out some disks that he slaps into the sampler and his Mac, saving the sample and giving it a name. Iago's already pulling out an old hardcore tune for the breakbeat. The hardness of it forcing a smile from me as I remember back in the days when I heard Acen's "Trip to the Moon, Part II" and said, That was the lick, that was the lick. That was my entrance into hardcore, or breakbeat house or whatever you want to call it. But back then it was just majestic.

I sit silent in the background as the palette of samples is collected, from Eddie Murphy doing his Mr T impression in *Delirious*, to a set of violins playing off Marvin Gaye's "Here My Dear." Watch Dean and Iago hunch forward over the Mac, editing the breakbeat, chopping it in half, then half again, making it off-beat and unrhythmical, then bringing it back, shortening its duration, lengthening it. Putting in a sub-bass underneath to give it a kick when it's played in the clubs. Deciding how long the intro should roll for. After a while it becomes cluttered with so many samples running into one another, a cacophony of sound. Then they pare it back, taking out an edit here, a sample there, merging them into one another until they create a unified whole. I lie slumped in the background, lying across Dean's bed, my eyes half closed. The nebulous underwater sounds rolling around me.

A sample, breaking through and making its presence felt, the tight drum pattern cut into another area, sharp and glinting, then disappearing away as the sub-bass rolls through. I lie there and I'm thinking, Why can't I do this? Me who's loved music for as long as I can remember, why can't I do this? The question becomes all-consuming. I know breaks, I know beats, why can't I do this?

Exhibition

I walk slowly down the road, my hands shoved deep into my pockets, my head lowered as day gives way to night. The golden hour all around me. That magical hour between sunset and darkness when everything has a magical glow. My shirt flutters in the breeze. I didn't know what to wear, didn't know how formal it would be. Just that the invitation had on it wine and cheese afterwards. What the hell that has to do with dressing up I don't know. But I decided to be smart casual, a baggy pair of chinos, a big old white cotton shirt, buttoned at the top but not the bottom, and some leather ankle boots that I only wear when I feel I have to look smart. My sunglasses cover my eyes, and I have no desire for anyone to look at me or notice me. Iago dropped me off and I was grateful. After last night's session with Dean, we haven't spoken much. Just sort of left the words festering between us. I want to sort it out but sometimes shit goes too far and before you know it it's careering out of control and you've lost it totally.

I stop for a second and look around me, trying to find the right street, pull out the card with its little map and directions. Turning it one way then the other. Looking up to check street names. Then, confident that I'm going in the right direction, walking again. I walk, but it's not my usual walking stride where I'm looking up and watching and seeing things, where I've got a place to go and I'm travelling towards it. This is a slower, more funereal walk, with my head down and a scowl on my face. This is: I don't want to talk to anyone ever. Just get out of my way and let me slip into the background. I had thought about not turning up. But I keep my promises and I want to see her again. I want to lust after her again, to see whether I have any energy and desire left, or if my losing the record has just shoved me into a thousand-year slump.

Stop outside of the gallery, it's got a big open glass front, about twenty by twenty feet. Light is coming out over the pavement, but it's coming through a huge off-white fabric sheet that is covering the whole entrance. A sign says that it is a private viewing by invitation only. Stand for a second trying to figure out how to get in. Step to the glass door that is in the centre of the front and look for a bell. Find a rather ornate little one, all crafted bronze, a little demon's head with its tongue sticking out. I press the tongue gingerly and hear the bell ring. The fabric is pulled aside, showing that it is in fact slit at the point over the door, and I am ushered in.

The guy on the door takes my invitation and offers me a drink from the table beside him.

"What would you like to drink? We have white wine or red. Or if you prefer, orange or apple juice."

"I'll have some red wine, thanx."

He hands me a large glass that is half filled with a gloriously scarlet red wine, which I sniff tentatively before taking a gulp of. The smell is reminiscent of strawberries and pears, and the taste is just overwhelming, so many different textures and flavours coming one after the other. Nod my head to him and move into the white interior, down a wide space, following the sounds of voices. Most of them middle class and I'm assuming white, as I haven't seen them yet. Turn a corner and see them, dressed casually in their designer labels, with their hands held high as they smoke their cigarettes and hold their drinks, sipping from them every now and then. My eyes are fixed on them as I step forwards sipping from my own glass of wine. Looking at them and trying to discern their ages, their careers, which of the women I find attractive. It's not until I'm a few feet away from them that I become aware of the images on the wall. Big black-and-white prints are set in rows along the walls, all of them about 20" by 20". I stare open-mouthed at them, then I start to laugh, not loud, just a little giggle to myself, and the broadest smile I've ever felt creases across my face.

Inez's exhibition consists of very large photos of male and female genitalia in various states of arousal. Looking at it reminds me of porno mags, but then again, a lot of things I see do that. But what makes me smile is the total irreverence of the images. How they seem to be taking the piss out of the reverence that society holds for sex and sexuality. I feel like saying, Yes, this is good and great, this is how sex should be shown. Sex as fun. But I content myself by walking along the lines of photos and looking at each one individually before moving on. Listening to the highbrow talk around me as I become the invisible man, apart from the crowd.

It takes me about fifteen minutes to get round the whole display. That's without reading the little plaques beside the photos. Just walking round and looking at them one after the other and deciding which ones I like and which ones I don't. As I finish my circular journey, finding that my wine has finished, I decide I like the opening picture more than any of the others. A very close shot of a vagina, with the outer lips pulled aside by painted nails and the words "Hello, big boy" typed across the opening.

I turn to get a refill of my wine and she's standing behind me in a cotton suit which is draped across her. Flowing and slightly oversized. I look at her and wonder whether she is wearing a bra.

"Do you like them?"

"Yes, I do. Very funny. How much do they cost?"

"It varies, between two and five hundred pounds."

I whistle.

"Shit! Does anyone buy them?"

"Yes. I think we've sold about half of the ones up now."

"How much money do you make a year?"

"Enough."

"Ask me how much I make."

"How much do you make?"

"About twelve grand a year, I'm told. Now do you make more or less than that?"

"More."

"Ah, a woman with money I see."

We're walking back towards the wine table as I lean close and nudge her with my elbow. She smiles and sips from her wine.

"How long did it take you to take all of those photos?"

"About a year. It wouldn't have taken so long if I'd been able to find the models I needed, but everyone's so shy in this country, it's unbelievable."

"So it was hard to find models then?"

"Yes. I had to put out advertisements, phone people, it took a long time."

"I would have thought there were plenty of people out there willing to get naked for photos?"

"You'd be surprised how few there really are. They might not mind you taking a photo of them bare-chested, but ask them to play with their dick and it becomes a bit more difficult."

I laugh loud, that raucous laugh that many people have told me many times to change as it is so loud and piercing that it makes people stop and stare and wonder what I'm laughing about. Inez looks at me for a second, but it doesn't faze her. We get to the wine table. I decide to have the white this time, and sip its chilled flavour down slowly.

"Joel says you've been having a hard time lately?"

I look at her and I can feel the cloud behind my eyes start to roll forward. I hadn't been aware of it, but just being in the exhibition, I hadn't thought about the record once. It hadn't affected me at all. But with the sudden interjection of it I can feel the pain coming back again.

"I don't want to talk about it. Just makes me depressed."

Inez links her arm through mine and I'm surprised. For a split second I feel to pull away before I think to ask myself what I'm doing. A very beautiful woman has just placed herself very close to you indeed and you want to move away? Get out of town! We walk back into the exhibition area and I listen as she talks about her work.

"I wanted to do some stuff on sex that wasn't clinical or degrading. From a female perspective. Just having fun with trying it. Taking out the embarrassment around it. Men are to a degree much more open with their sexual organs 'cause they are all out in the open. Women have to search to find ours. Female examination is such a private thing, I wanted to make it open and freer. Moving away from that stigma that is attached to it. The stigma that is attached to a woman's interior."

We're stopped in front of a picture with a woman examining herself by looking in a CD, using it as if it were a mirror.

"You know men can just fragmentalise women; we're just breasts or legs, or arse or faces. We become fractured, never whole human beings, because we're always the passive ones, the ones who wait. I wanted to show women being assertive in their sexuality and not just being one thing or another but a unified whole."

"Pretty passionate about this, aren't you?"

"I'm a woman, I have to be. If I don't change it, who will? Men won't, they're too happy with the status quo."

"Sweeping generalisation there."

"Why not? Men have been doing it for years, making all women into mothers or whores. There's more to women than that."

"Am I placed into that categorisation of men?"

"Yes."

"Shit, you be hard."

"Not all women have to be nurturers."

"Yeah, but you also have to understand that all men aren't bastards. Men are changing just as women are."

"But not fast enough, too many of you are stuck in that Neanderthal way of thinking of women as just being sexual objects, vessels to fill."

"Yeah, but acting like a lad doesn't mean that we can't still question and wonder about it, but it also means that maybe we just can't evolve that fast. Because it doesn't matter you saying tear down the old stereotypes, because there is nothing to take their place, so what are we supposed to be if you can't tell us and what we were before is wrong?"

"You're supposed to be able to treat women with respect and not to act as if the world belongs to you. To understand that requires a development that men don't want to face; it means opening yourselves up to the fact that you are not invulnerable and that you can feel emotional pain."

"Men have been opening themselves up to emotional pain

for a long time. Women just have to understand that they don't know men. They might think they know, but you don't know men at all. And that the 'All men are bastards' line don't work."

"That's your point of view."

"Yep, it is."

We pause.

"Looks like we'll never get along."

"You can say that again."

We stand there quietly in front of the photo. Me thinking I've definitely blown it here. Mum would have been proud of me though for holding up my end of the argument so well. Even though I know she'd be on Inez's side.

"What are you doing after this?"

I'm surprised by the question.

"Nothing much, go home, maybe make a few tapes."

"Do you want to get something to eat?"

"Wouldn't mind. Are you a veggie?"

"No, are you?"

"No."

"Good."

"Where do you want to eat?"

"There's a really good Mexican place not far from here."

"How would we get there? My friend dropped me off, and I'm not a great one for public transport."

"My car's parked out front."

"Don't you have to be here until the end."

"They won't miss me."

We slip outside and she walks over to a Fiat Punto convertible parked up by the kerb. It's that bright golden metallic yellow you see on the ads and you wonder what in heaven made them decide to create a colour like that. She skips lightly round to the driver's door and I hear the central locking open with a clunk. Slide in and she's already pulling away from the kerb, her short hair rustling across her neck as the wind pushes against us. She drives fast and sure, like Iago, but without heart-pounding fear and the intense doses of adrenalin. Her hands light on the wheel as she changes gear.

"The last time I saw you, you were using a cane. What was wrong with your leg?"

"Hasn't Joel told you yet?"

"No."

"Jason Milson, the A&R director for Zefal, took me off my bike while I was working."

"Working as what?"

"A courier."

"You're a courier?"

"Used to be. My knee's getting better, but I haven't ridden a bike since, so I don't know whether I can go back to it. But being an A&R man isn't my idea of heaven at this moment in time, so I'll have to see what happens."

"What's wrong with being an A&R man? Joel loves it."

"I don't think I'm able to kiss arse as much as Joel can. I'd rather not have some artist complaining about the water not being hot enough in their room and things to that affect. I'd tell them to sort it out themselves and stop being such a baby. I'm not here to take care of people who are old enough to take care of themselves."

"So you don't think you've got a future in it?"

"No, not really. It's difficult, because the music I might want to sign they have no interest in and no understanding of. So there's not much I can do until I learn how to make them understand."

"What music would you like to sign?"

"Anything black: jungle, jazz funk, soul, hip hop, ragga. Anything and everything. It's just…"

I make a flapping gesture in the air and retreat into silence.

We pull up to some lights and a Porsche pulls up alongside, looks like a Carrera 4, with the small rear wing. The driver looks across and starts preening as soon as his eyes spot Inez. His foot throbs on his accelerator, the engine of the Porsche, growling as he tweaks it. Inez looks towards him, up and down, then brings her eyes back onto the road. The lights change and he's away, engine roaring, his taillights becoming a flicker in the distance. Before Inez pulls away at a moderate pace.

"Do you get that sort of attention all the time?"

"Yeah, you learn to live with it after a while."

"Do you think of yourself as beautiful?"

"I try not to, you know. Just think of myself as attractive, with bits that I don't like, but when men keep telling you, and people keep telling you, that you're beautiful, you start to believe the hype. You fall into this spiral of 'They think I'm beautiful so I must be beautiful,' and then that's the only thing that matters. My outward appearance."

"I know what you mean."

"I don't think any man can. Your whole life isn't dominated by the need to be attractive to the other sex. Ugly men still get beautiful women, but you don't really see it working in reverse. And apart from that, men can be good at things that have no bearing on their physical appearance, whereas women are dominated by it."

She pauses for breath.

"Is our conversation going to be like this all night?"

"I think so."

Nineties Girl

I've thought about this moment a lot. How I would approach it. What it would be like. But it's here now and I still don't know what I should be doing. It is this way every time with someone new. The uncertainty of being with someone, of not knowing where they like to be touched, how they like to be touched, what sort of sexual person they are.

We had dinner at this marvellous Mexican place, over the speakers was a constant Latin rhythm, samba, mambo. The place was throbbing, not just with the music but with people. This was a place to which people enjoyed coming. Voices were raised loud as tequila was downed. Lick the salt, down the liquor, bite the lime. In the open kitchen area in the centre of the restaurant, where the smell of food was just overpowering, you could see the food you'd just ordered being prepared before your eyes. See the flames spilling forth from the gas burners. The rattle of pans and the shouting of voices as the cooks weaved in and out of each other, moving from place to place. Knives in their hands as they chopped meat or diced vegetables. Just adding to the chaotic noisy atmosphere. But the most wonderful thing about the restaurant was the smell. As soon as you entered you could smell the food. My mouth was watering before I'd even sat down. I wanted to eat. We talked, but I could see the place was having the same effect on Inez. We found that people ordered almost immediately upon entering this restaurant, whereas usually they would wait a little while, discussing the menu and sipping their drinks, talking and waiting for the waitress to get round to them. Here people would grab a menu and a waiter upon entering and force them to take their order, with the intoxicating aroma swimming in our nostrils.

Whilst our stomachs rumbled and the wondrous smells engulfed us from the kitchen, we talked, or rather she talked and I listened. Interjecting a story here or a point there. It is, my mother says, one of my more feminine traits, the ability to listen and be captivated by what a person is saying and seem interested whether I am or not. She says I make people feel like they could tell me anything.

So I sat and listened, truly listened to her speak about her childhood in Hong Kong and Jamaica, her father's love of music and the label that he runs. How he went from small-time survivor to a major force on the reggae scene. How her mother loves pottery and spends most of her time making strange sculptures of her dreams, and how she spends so much time travelling between Jamaica and Hong Kong. How when she was nine, Inez was sent to stay with family on her mother's side in London and was educated here. Losing her broad Jamaican accent but not her love of dub or rum, which she drank as a child. When she would follow her grandfather down to the local rum shop and he would sit her on his knee and she would sip from his glass.

I find out that she's an Aquarius, loves baseball and hates to cook, though she can rather well. That if she could be reincarnated she'd come back as a killer whale. That she hates the Conservatives as much as I do, but several of her close friends are card-carrying Tories. That we enjoy the same taste in music, that she cares not a whit for football and that in her past twenty-four years she has had seven boyfriends, and two of those were for a year or more. That she is single now, has a belly button that is curved inward, likes to be kissed behind the ear, and that she is very sensitive along the outer curve of her thigh.

I kiss her neck and whisper in her ear.

"Mina! Mina!"

She pushes me away, looking into my face.

"What did you say?"

"Mina! Mina!"

"Who's Mina?"

"She's Dracula's lost love, who he pines for. I say it because I vant to vite your neck."

She laughs, and I've never been so glad to hear someone laugh before in my life. I bend forward and bite her gently on her neck, feel her hand slid up my shirt and tiptoe its way along my spine. Caressing each vertebrae in turn.

"Do you give good massage?"

"I give very good massage."

"Hhhmmmm! You'll have to give me one sometime."

"You can give me one right now."

She laughs huskily in my ear at her joke, and I smile with her. She tugs at my buttons and slides my shirt off. Her hands roving across my bare skin.

"I want you to be naked first."

I don't know what she's going to say when she sees the bruising along my side and I'm already steeling myself for any words that she says. She says nothing, her fingers tracing the edges of the bruising before her mouth tenderly kisses every inch of flesh that is bruised. Her kisses so soft and thrilling.

My shirt is still around my wrists and she pulls it off before throwing it into a corner of my room. I'm flipped on to my back as she tackles my buttons. Her fingers pulling at them, popping them open one by one, before she slides my chinos down my legs, her cheek, following slowly behind the fabric, rubbing itself against my hairy legs. She gives them a sharp tug and I hear them fall into a heap on the floor. Look down and see her hands sliding up my thighs to gently tug at the waistbands of my boxers, peeling them away from my groin as I raise my butt to help her slide them down. They fall onto the floor with a flutter, but then I'm being engulfed by her mouth as she leans over me and it's all I can do to breathe as she teases me.

I hold her head gently and pull her towards me, she slides along my body, the fabric of her suit rough on my newly sensitised flesh me. I kiss her. Smelling my scent on her face.

I pull her off the bed, she's surprised, her mouth open as I lean her against the wall and spread her legs and arms. I lean close against her, rubbing my nakedness against the fabric of her suit. My hands move from her ankles down her arms to her chest, rubbing over her breasts, cupping them, feeling them swell slightly within my palms and her nipples stiffen and lengthen. Skim my fingers across her stomach and then down her inner thighs. Place my hand against her, feel the heat emanating from inside, feel her breath stop.

As I bend my knees and slide my hands along her thighs, down around her calves, with my head rubbing against her backside, move my hands in slow circles up her legs while I bite her through the suit, hearing her yelp in surprise.

Turn her around and quickly pull her out of her suit, I want her to be as naked as I am as quickly as I am. Strip her of her clothes and pull her against me naked. We kiss and it feels like I'm being slowly turned into jelly, a quivering mass of uncontrollability. I jerk against her stomach.

"What was that?"

"What was what?"

I jerk again, uncontrollably.

"That."

"Oh, you mean this?"

I flex again and she smiles, holding it gently in her palm. I turn her towards the long mirror on the wall and hold her. I lean over her and we look into the mirror, my darkness against her paleness. Masculinity around femininity. I kiss her neck and my hand cups her breast. She turns in my arms and kisses me, and I stagger backwards onto the bed, still holding onto her. We fall and she lands on me, knocking the wind out of me for a second. Turn us around and kiss her neck, leaning over her. Leaving a trail of heated saliva as I weave a path from her neck around her breasts, my mouth encompassing her nipples. Sucking, making her arch her back and hold my head close before starting once more on my exploration down across her stomach, leaving a pool of fluid in her belly button, then down through her hair and down along her slit. Opening her with my tongue and gently licking and nuzzling. How long I'm down here for I know not, just that I feel her hands hold my head and pull me upwards as if I were underwater and drowning. I slide back up her body, my lips kissing as much of her flesh as possible before I reach her, my eyes looking into hers.

I kiss her, smearing her liquid across her lips and cheeks, smelling her twice, her own perfume, intensely provocative and arousing and the soft scent underneath of her skin, slightly musky with a sheen of sweat. I reach out a hand a grab the box of condoms. tearing frantically at them, trying to get one out. She takes it from me and opens it with ease, before, sliding it over me and pulling me inside her. She bends her knees and I am so deep inside her I want to cry; her face creases then clears every time I enter her. I shift slightly and we stop.

"What was that?"

"I heard it too."

I push gently forward and then slightly faster, and we hear it again, a loud flatulent sound. I look her dead in the eye, and she cracks up, followed a split second later by me. Her legs unfold and we lie joined, laughing until we cry at the sound of the infamous fanny fart.

Full Circle

I sit in my room and watch Inez shift under my sheets. Her body glazed in the moonlight. The softness of it giving an ethereal beauty to her. The softness of her features as she sleeps endearing her even more to me. I lean precariously back in the director's chair and spark-up the spliff that I hold in my hand, inhaling deep of its fragrant aroma and letting the smoke settle in my lungs.

I lounge here for a while just watching her. Wondering whether she is the one. Maybe she is, maybe, she isn't. But I know right now that I don't feel uncomfortable with her being here. If she were to lie here forever, I would feel comfortable with her.

I stub out the spliff as the roach glows red hot and ease myself out of the chair, moving over to my collection. Quietly so as not to wake her, going through the records beneath my fingertips. Taking out one here or there, putting others back in their correct placing. Until a small pile sits beside me of records I want to listen to.

Tomorrow, or the next day, I'm going to drag Iago to Dean's and we are going to make the living track. Then I'm going to see whether I can get Dean signed to Zefal. I might as well do something while I'm there. See if I can break jungle into the mainstream. White people can't continue to walk around with their heads in the sand and continue to disregard the vibrancy that black culture brings to their lives. Paying lip service through adverts that have a crap rap or some bastardised version of "Incredible" for an air freshener. Maybe it's my duty to make sure that the contribution by black culture isn't ever overlooked. Then again, I might just make lots of fucking money out of it then run like hell. But either way I'm in it for the long haul.

I slide the records into my Timbuk2 and stand, looking at the shirts up on the wall. What has so drastically changed in the past few days to drag me out of the pit I was lying in. Can it be so simple that you find someone you're attracted to, fuck your brains out and everything that was bad suddenly rights itself and you become once more a happy camper? I reach up and pull on my shirt, feeling that luminous feeling engulf me as that wondrous fabric slides over my skin.

Sit back down in the director's chair and watch Inez some more. Pull out my last spliff and light it up. Savouring the lungfuls of sweet intoxication, blowing out fragrant incense into the night.

Inez shifts, her eyelids flicker as her arm stretches out, stroking the warm space where I was. She lifts her head, sleep still lying smooth across her features. Her eyes half opened.

"Whuh?"

I wonder whether she's going to wake up fully or just slip back into slumberland. Her eyes widen and she snaps awake. Her head searching for me, stopping when she sees me sitting at the end of the bed.

"What time is it?"

"Don't know, three, maybe four."

"What are you doing?"

"Smoking."

She rubs her eyes and brings herself fully awake, leaning forwards. Tugging the sheet underneath her armpits and across her breasts. She stretches out her hand, fingers extended and I lean forward giving her the spliff. She pulls on it, her lips becoming and O, the smooth smoke slipping from her lips as she breathes out. Her nostrils flaring as she breathes. The red tip glowing in front of her mouth. She runs a hand through her shortened hair, as if she's still got longer tresses, before bringing it down to smooth over the creases of the sheet. I hand her an ashtray, but she waves it away, handing the spliff back to me. I take it and tug on it again.

"What happened at the club that night?"

The question stops me in mid-drag and I have to consciously tell myself to keep inhaling, as my diaphragm tightens. I take my time in exhaling and let the question sit between us as I think about how to answer it.

"I heard a tune that I hadn't heard in a long time."

I start out slow, the tension still there, the pain still there. The grief I felt over the loss of the record making my words slow and tentative. I've always had trouble communicating how I felt. I'd try and talk about it and it would be like someone had clamped their hand over my throat and I'd be unable to speak. Just unable to get the words out of my throat. That's how it is now. My mouth moving but words not coming out.

Silence is between us, though it doesn't feel like an uncomfortable one. I take another drag on the spliff and blow it out slow, letting the drug take away my fears.

"I hadn't heard it in ten years. It was one of the defining things in my life, you know? What was it like the first time you held a camera and took a photo and knew that was what you wanted to do, more than anything else? When I heard that record, I knew, absolutely, that I wanted to be a DJ."

She listens, her eyes locked on me. Her whole body very still. Like a statue. But I'm only now and then sneaking glances at her, I'm too busy staring at the ground, at my hands, at my spliff, anything to avoid looking at her, making eye contact.

"So I haven't heard it for ten years and then I hear it again and it's like, I've got to find out what it's called, because I never knew. Never knew the name of this record that changed my life. It was like I was possessed, everything else was shut out. So I left you, didn't even know what I was doing standing in front of you. The alarms went off, water starting coming down, but I didn't care, I had to have that record. That name. Got to the DJ booth and he's packing everything away, and there I am asking him what the record was called. Like any person with any sense would do, he ignored me. I tried to get the name, but he wasn't having any of it. We tussled and I got left in the water, listening to the fire engines arrive."

I tug again on the spliff and find that it's nothing but roach. Look around and find my rolling equipment and quickly roll one while I continue my sad, pathetic story.

"I started searching for it."

Put the spliff in my mouth and light it.

"It's called 'One Last Time' and it's by Julianne Wilson and Fred Wesley. There aren't any copies over here, they only printed up about five or six, and they're all in the States. And I'm never going to hear it again."

I sit there tugging on the spliff and finally get the nerve up to look into her eye and stay looking in her eye. She tilts her head to one side and smiles gently. A twinkle developing in her eye.

"Men are funny."

I can feel something building inside of me, but I don't know what it is. I've just poured out my heart to this woman and all she can say is that men are funny.

She gets out of my bed, her olive skin silver in the moonlight.

The dark V of her crotch attracting my eye, as do her breasts, pert and luscious with her nipples erect and upstanding. She steps across to me and holds out her hand. I take it and she pulls me to her and hugs me. And whatever was building up inside of me disappears. Like Tommy Cooper would say, just like that.

"Funny ha ha or funny strange?"

"Funny strange."

I pull away from her and move over to my shirts on the wall, taking one down and giving it to her.

"Put it on."

She does, and it never looked as good on me as it does on her. Reaching down to just below her crotch. She sits on the end of my bed and I can see the dark curly hairs between her thighs.

"I still feel the pain now. I want that record so much, sometimes it's hard to breathe for the pain."

"Do I make it easier to handle?"

"I don't know. I know when I'm with you, I'm not thinking about the record, and I don't sense the pain. But I know it's lurking down there, and that it could overtake me again, if I'm not careful."

"People live with pain, and over time its ability to hurt you diminishes until it's just a dull ache and then it's gone."

"That doesn't make it any easier to live with now."

"Nope, but nobody said life was easy."

I step over to her and kiss her on the neck, just above the fabric of my Brazil top. Using my weight to press her back onto my bed.

"What do you want to listen to? D'Angelo, Jodeci, Roberta Flack, Bill Withers, Curtis Mayfield, Me'shell N'degeochello?"

She kisses me to make me stop talking, and I do. The record just a dull murmur in the back of my mind.

Thanks!

HOW DO YOU WRITE ONE OF THESE THANK-YOU LISTS WITHOUT SOUNDING LIKE A KNOB WHOSE ONLY DESIRE IS TO NAME AS MANY PEOPLE THAT YOU KNOW SO THAT YOU DON'T CATCH FLAK FROM THEM WHEN THEY READ THE BOOK AND SAY, HEY, HOW COMES YOU DIDN'T THANK ME?

THEN OF COURSE YOU GET THE VERY WEAK, THANKS TO EVERYONE THAT KNOWS ME, WHICH IS JUST SO MUCH WANK. BECAUSE EVERYONE THAT KNOWS YOU DIDN'T HAVE MUCH OF AN IMPACT ON WHAT YOU WERE WRITING ANYWAY.

BUT HEY, IT'S IN MY CONTRACT SO:
'NUFF LOVE TO

CEE	ANN
HERBS	AILEEN
EDDIE	KARL
DEBBIE	JOHN
RICKY	LESLIE
LUCIA	AMANDA
STEPHANIE	MUNROE
FIZZ	OLIVE
DIVYA	WAYNE
LINDA	MANOJ
JADE	CRAIG
FRAN	TREVOR
RYAN	AND ALL THE MASSIVE.
MICHAEL	
COLLEEN	

BIG SHOUT TO THE MANY PEOPLE AT TOUCH AND TRUE, WHO OFTEN WONDER WHO THAT NIGGA WITH THE GLASSES IS WHEN I WANDER THROUGH THEIR OFFICES.

RESPECT DUE TO FIONA HUSTON AND ROB MELBOURNE FOR THEIR INFORMATION AND THE TIME THEY GAVE ME AS I TRIED TO RESEARCH THIS BOOK YOU HOLD IN YOUR HANDS.

HAVE TO SAY THANKS TO JAKE LINGWOOD, WHO WAS COOL AND CALM UNDER PRESSURE.

AND THEN THERE'S THE FAMILY. MUM, DAD, JACKIE AND RASHANA. I DO LOVE YOU ALL.

PEACE OUT, UNTIL THE NEXT TIME.

"ALL THAT IS REQUIRED FOR EVIL TO TRIUMPH IS THAT GOOD PEOPLE DO NOTHING"

PLAYLIST
(IN NO PARTICULAR ORDER)

D'ANGELO, "BROWN SUGAR"
BLACKBYRDS, "ROCKCREEK PARK"
NOTORIOUS BIG, "ONE MORE CHANCE"
FAITH, "YOU USED TO LOVE ME"
MARY J. BLIGE, "MY LIFE"
ALKAHOLIKS, "MAKE ROOM"
PHARCYDE, "RUBBER SONG"
D'ANGELO, "CRUISIN'"
ME'SHELL, "IF THAT'S YOUR BOYFRIEND, HE WASN'T
    LAST NIGHT"
DONALD BYRD, "PLACES AND SPACES"
BLACK MOON, "BUCK 'EM DOWN"
HOUSE OF PAIN, "ON POINT"
OLD DIRTY BASTARD, "SHIMMY SHIMMY"
WU-TANG CLAN, "PROTECT YA NECK"
METHOD MAN, "BRING THE PAIN"
OHIO PLAYERS, "FIRE"
THE O'JAYS, "FOR THE LOVE OF MONEY"
DIONNE FARRIS, "NOW OR LATER"
LENNY KRAVITZ, "SUGAR"
JADE, "EVERYTHING"
MARVIN GAYE, "COME LIVE WITH ME ANGEL"
JUNIOR MAFIA, "PLAYER'S ANTHEM"
A TRIBE CALLED QUEST, "AWARD TOUR"

KWEST, "A HUNDRED AND ONE THINGS TO DO WHILE
I'M WITH YOUR GIRL"
MOBB DEEP, "DRINK AWAY THE PAIN"
MISS JONES, "IT AIN'T GONNA BE BOY"
BRANDY, "BABY"
NAUGHTY BY NATURE, "CRAZIEST"
ONYX, "LIVE"
JUICY, "SUGAR FREE"
SWEET CHARLES, "YES IT'S YOU"
JAMES BROWN, "BLUES AND PANTS"
MASSIVE ATTACK, "PROTECTION"
DEEP BLUE, "THE HELICOPTER TUNE"
OLD DIRTY BASTARD, "BROOKLYN ZOO"
JODECI, "FEENIN"
BARRY WHITE, "SO MUCH LOVE TO GIVE"
WHITEHEAD BROS, "FORGET I WAS A G"

JUNGLIST

JAMES T KIRK
& TWO FINGAS

Back in print after two decades, *Junglist* tells the compelling, comic, stream-of-consciousness story of four young Black men coming of age among the raves and Jungle music scene in London during the 1990s.

Layered with poetic verse, prose and humour, this cult classic of underground British fiction documents the rollercoaster ride of a weekend spent raving during Jungle's cultural takeover in the summer of 1994. Jungle, with its booming basslines and Jamaican patois, burst from the pirate radio stations and mixtapes into cavernous clubs, pulling a generation of Black British ravers with it. Originally written as a way to document street culture as it became a feature of London, charting a time when working-class kids, both Black and white, merged to dance as "one family", *Junglist* is both a testament to Black British sound system culture and a rawthentic account of inner-city life.

Order online from RepeaterBooks.com

SPIRIT BEHIND THE LENS:

THE MAKING OF A HIP-HOP PHOTOGRAPHER

EDDIE OTCHERE

Spirit Behind the Lens is a reminder that photographic narratives are the bedrock of photography. Its intimacy is borne from the printed material that defined the history of contemporary black culture. A whole life on film, curated by pivotal moments donated from the past. The photography of today is taken from the journals of yesterday. The visual world of one of hip-hop's most enigmatic photographers, Eddie Otchere.

Hailing from the epicentre of London's jungle scene, this book documents how Otchere crafted the visual identities of house, garage, jungle, drum n bass and hip-hop, working with artists including lil Louis, So Solid Crew, Kemet Crew, Goldie and Black Star.

Order online from RepeaterBooks.com

PETER BRÖTZMANN:

FREE-JAZZ, REVOLUTION & THE POLITICS OF IMPROVISATION

DANIEL SPICER

Peter Brötzmann explores the heroic life and revolutionary music of the pioneering German saxophonist, and the radical social and political convictions that informed them. Drawing on extensive interviews with Brötzmann and key associates, it traces the German saxophonist's crucial role as a pioneer of European free jazz, his restless travels and collaborations and his eventual superstardom, examining the life and work of a fiercely uncompromising artist with a reputation for gruff intensity and total commitment.

The first ever, full-length, English-language biography of one of the most fascinating and inspiring personalities in the history of Western improvised music. Both intimate and wide-ranging, it tells the story of a man and a music that changed the world.

MIXING POP AND POLITICS: A MARXIST HISTORY OF POPULAR MUSIC

TOBY MANNING

A radical history of the political and social upheavals of the last 70 years, told through the period's most popular music. *Mixing Pop and Politics* is not a history of political music, but a political history of popular music. Spanning the early 50s to the present, it shows how, from doo-wop to hip-hop, punk to crunk and grunge to grime, music has both reflected and resisted the political events of its era.

It explores the connections between popular music and political ideology, whether that's the liberation of rock'n'roll or the containment of girl groups, the refusal of glam or the resignation of soft rock, the solidarity of disco or the individualism of 80s pop.

Order online from RepeaterBooks.com

LIKE LOCKDOWN NEVER HAPPENED: MUSIC AND CULTURE DURING COVID

JOY WHITE

During the COVID-19 pandemic, music listening increased as people used it to help to counter the psychological fallout of lockdown and reduce its effects of isolation, restriction and boredom. At the same time, concerts and other musical events moved online, and even when lockdown eased, social distancing meant that group musical and cultural events took on a different format.

With a focus on contemporary Black music, this book takes a deep dive into a few of the various forms that popular culture took over this period, including Kano's Newham Talks series; Steve McQueen's BBC anthology *Small Axe*; the Verzuz DJ Battle series; TikTok's Don't Rush Challenge; radio station theresnosignal; and many more.

Order online from RepeaterBooks.com

REPEATER BOOKS

is dedicated to the creation of a new reality. The landscape of twenty-first-century arts and letters is faded and inert, riven by fashionable cynicism, egotistical self-reference and a nostalgia for the recent past. Repeater intends to add its voice to those movements that wish to enter history and assert control over its currents, gathering together scattered and isolated voices with those who have already called for an escape from Capitalist Realism. Our desire is to publish in every sphere and genre, combining vigorous dissent and a pragmatic willingness to succeed where messianic abstraction and quiescent co-option have stalled: abstention is not an option: we are alive and we don't agree.